Nikki Logan lives next to a string of protected wetlands in Western Australia, with her long-suffering partner and a menagerie of furred, feathered and scaly mates. She studied film and theatre at university, and worked for years in advertising and film distribution before finally settling down in the wildlife industry. Her romance with nature goes way back, and she considers her life charmed, given she works with wildlife by day and writes fiction by night—the perfect way to combine her two loves. Nikki believes that the passion and risk of falling in love are perfectly mirrored in the danger and beauty of wild places. Every romance she writes contains an element of nature, and if readers catch a waft of rich earth or the spray of wild ocean between the pages she knows her job is done.

Visit Nikki at her website: www.nikkilogan.com.au

Praise for
Nikki Logan:

'Superb debut—4.5 stars.'
—*RT Book Reviews* on
LIGHTS, CAMERA…KISS THE BOSS!

'Now, here is an Australian writer
who manages to both tell a good story and to
capture Australia well. I had fun from start to finish.
Nikki Logan will be one to watch.'
—*www.goodreads.com* on
LIGHTS, CAMERA…KISS THE BOSS!

'This story has well-defined and soundly motivated
characters as well as a heart-wrenching conflict.'
—*RT Book Reviews* on
THEIR NEWBORN GIFT

RAPUNZEL IN NEW YORK

BY

NIKKI LOGAN

All the characters in this book have no existence outside the imagination of the author, and have no relation whatsoever to anyone bearing the same name or names. They are not even distantly inspired by any individual known or unknown to the author, and all the incidents are pure invention.

First published in Great Britain 2011
by Mills & Boon, an imprint of Harlequin (UK) Limited,
Eton House, 18-24 Paradise Road, Richmond, Surrey TW9 1SR

ISBN: 978 0 263 22052 0

Harlequin (UK) policy is to use papers that are natural, renewable and recyclable products and made from wood grown in sustainable forests. The logging and manufacturing process conform to the legal environmental regulations of the country of origin.

Printed and bound in Great Britain
by CPI Antony Rowe, Chippenham, Wiltshire

Also by Nikki Logan:

A KISS TO SEAL THE DEAL
SHIPWRECKED WITH MR WRONG
LIGHTS, CAMERA…KISS THE BOSS
THEIR NEWBORN GIFT
SEVEN-DAY LOVE STORY
THE SOLDIER'S UNTAMED HEART
FRIENDS TO FOREVER

Did you know these are also available as eBooks?
Visit www.millsandboon.co.uk

Dedication

To Carol and Marlon: I hope my Viktoria is the kind of woman you'd have wanted yours to grow into.

Acknowledgement

To my friend Sandra Galati, and coffee-shop stranger Teresa Izzard, for your invaluable assistance discovering Manhattan. Sandra and I were meeting in a coffee shop halfway around the world from Morningside, NY, where this book is set, and the woman at the next table had lived there for a year. Talk about kismet!

And to all the internet sites dedicated to New York City's urban raptors. Thank you! I had a wonderful time researching this story and watching your beautiful birds every day.

CHAPTER ONE

"You'd better get up here, Nathan. There's a woman about to jump from your building."

Two sentences.

That's all it took to tear Nathan Archer away from his Columbus Circle office and send him racing uptown. Ironic that the A-line was quicker than a cab or even his driver could get him up to Morningside, but the subway spilled him out just one block from the West 126th Street building he'd grown up in. Grown old in. Well before his time.

He pushed through the gathered throng, shaking his head at the impatient crowd. Was there a whole population of people who hovered in alleys and bars just waiting for some poor individual to be nudged too far in life? To climb out onto a bridge or a rooftop?

Or a ledge.

He followed their collective gaze upward. Sure enough, there she was. Not exactly preparing for a swan dive; more crouched than standing. She looked young, though it was hard to tell from this distance.

She was staring at the sky with an intensity strong enough to render her completely oblivious to the crowd gathering below. He lifted his eyes to the popcorn clouds. Was she praying? Or was she just in her own tormented world?

"The crisis team is mobilizing," a nearby cop said, turning back to stare uselessly up to the tenth floor. "ETA twenty minutes."

Twenty minutes? She'd already been out there at least the quarter hour it had taken him to get uptown. The chances of her lasting another twenty?

Not high.

He glanced around at the many spectators who were doing exactly nothing to rectify the situation and swallowed a groan. There was a reason he was more of a behind-the-scenes kind of guy. Behind the scenes had served him well his whole life. You got a lot done when you weren't wasting time as the center of attention. He paid people to do the limelight thing.

Unfortunately, none of them were here.

He was.

Nathan looked back up at the looming building and the woman perched precariously on it. Hadn't these old walls contained enough misery?

He muttered a curse and his legs started moving. Had nobody thought of doing this sooner? He pushed past a gaggle of onlookers and headed toward the building, counting windows as he went. It took him three minutes to get into his own building and up to the eighth floor, and he passed three residents on the stairs up to the tenth—they had no clue about the drama unfolding in their own building. If they saw it on the news tonight they'd be kicking themselves they missed it. Not that it was making the news tonight, or any night while he still breathed. His development didn't need the bad press. He hadn't worked on it all this time only to have it turned upside down by a woman with a blown psychiatric fuse.

Nate burst through the stairwell door and turned left, counting the windows he knew to be on the outside of the building. *Nine...ten...eleven...*On twelve, he paused for only a second before delivering a strategic kick right at the weak point in the door of apartment 10B. As fragile as the rest of the century old building, it exploded inwards in a shower of splinters.

Inside, the apartment was neat and carefully decorated but

small enough that he was able to check all the five rooms in less than thirty seconds, even with a limp from the jar that had just about snapped his ankle. Three rooms had outside windows that were sealed tight—safety measures. But, apparently back at the turn of the twentieth century some architect had considered that only grown men needed to be saved from themselves, because every apartment had one more window—small and awkwardly positioned above the toilet cistern, but just big enough for a slight woman to wiggle through. Or a young boy.

He knew that from experience.

This one stood wide open, its tasteful lemon curtains blowing gently in the breeze, providing access onto 10B's sheltered ledge.

Nathan's heart hammered from way more than the urgent sprint up two flights of stairs. He took a deep, tense breath, climbed onto the closed lid of the toilet and peered out the window, sickeningly prepared to find nothing but pigeon droppings and a swirl of air where a woman had just been.

But she was still out there, her back to him as she stretched out on the ledge on all fours, giving him a great view of her denim-clad behind…

…and the tangle of ropes and rigging that fixed her more than securely to the ledge.

Frustrated fury bubbled up deep inside. Of all the stupid-ass, time-wasting stunts… He boosted himself up and half through the window and barked to her butt, "Honey, you'd better be planning to jump, or I'm going to throw you off here myself."

Viktoria Morfitt spun so fast she nearly lost her careful balance on the ledge. Her reflexes were dulled through lack of use, but her muscle memory was still entirely intact, and it choreographed her muscles now to brace her more securely on the narrow stone shelf. Adrenaline pulsed through her bloodstream and her lungs sucked in an ache of cold air and then expelled it on a ripe curse as she spotted the man wedged in her bathroom window glaring at her like a maniac. His voice had drawn her attention, but his words whooshed away on the relentless New York sounds coming up from Morningside's streets.

What the—? She shuffled backward as far as the ledge allowed and knocked against the peregrine nest box she'd just been installing.

The stranger lurched farther forward, half hanging out the window, enormous hands stretched out toward her, and spoke more clearly. More slowly. "Easy, honey. Just a joke. How about you come back inside now?"

She wasn't fooled by those treacle tones for one moment. Or the intense eyes. Bad guys never turned up at your doorstep badly scarred, carrying violin cases and talking like Robert deNiro. They turned up like this: nice shirt, open collar, careless hair and designer stubble. Big, well-manicured hands. Good-looking. Exactly the sort of guy you'd think was okay to let inside your apartment.

Except that he'd already let himself in.

For one crazy second Tori considered leaping off the ledge. Her intruder could help himself to her stuff—whatever he wanted—and she could lower herself down to Barney's ledge. He'd be home for sure and his bathroom window was perpetually open so he could smoke out of it. Her hand slipped to the titanium fixings at her pelvis. Her rigging would hold. It always did.

A sharp pain gnawed deep and low. *Almost always.*

She raised her voice instead, hoping to alert a neighbour. "How about you get the heck out of my apartment!" Tension thumped out of her in waves that translated into quavers in her voice. Could he tell?

He reached forward again. "Look—"

Tori slid hard up against the corner of the building, clambering around the nest box. Dammit, any farther and she'd knock it off the ledge and have to start all over again. Well, that and possibly kill someone walking below...

She glanced easily over the ledge and met the intense stares of thirty or so passersby and a couple of NYPD officers. "Hey!"

she yelled down to the cops. "Get up here! There's a burglar in my apartment—10B!"

The stranger surged through the window and made a grab for her foot. She kicked it away, then stole a moment to glance back down. Two of the cops were running towards her building.

Heat poured off the contemptuous look he shot at her. "You know what? I have a meeting to get back to. So either go ahead and jump or get the hell back in here." With that, he disappeared back into her apartment.

Jump? She glanced back down at the crowd below, their expectant faces all peering up. *At her.*

Oh…no!

Heat surged up her throat. Someone must have called her in as a jumper when she was out on the ledge. *He* thought she was a jumper. But while most of them stood below waiting for the aerial show, only one had had the nerve to race up here and actually try to help her.

He deserved points for that.

"Wait!"

She scrabbled toward the now-vacant window and crouched to look inside. He was taller than he looked when he was squashed through her tiny window—broader, too—and he completely filled the doorway to her bathroom. Self-preservation made her pause. Him being good-looking didn't change the fact he was a stranger. And she wasn't much on strangers.

Tori peered in at him. "I'll come in when you're not there."

He rolled his eyes, then found hers again. "Fine. I'll be in the hall."

Then he was gone.

She swiveled on her bottom and slid her legs quickly through the tiny window, stretching down until her feet hit the toilet lid. Then she unclipped her brace-line with the ease of years of practice, clenched her abs, and brought her torso through in a twist that would have been right at home in Cirque du Soleil.

As good as his word, he'd moved out into the very public hallway. But between them lay a forest of timber shards.

"You kicked in my *door*?" She hit a pitch she usually heard only from the peregrine falcons that circled her building looking for somewhere to raise their chicks.

A frustrated breath shot from between his thin lips. "Apologies for assuming you were about to die."

He didn't look the slightest bit apologetic, but he did look stunningly well-dressed and gorgeous, despite the aloof arch of his eyebrows. Just then two uniformed officers exploded through the fire-escape doors and bolted toward them.

"He kicked in my door!" Tori repeated for their benefit.

Taller than either of the cops, he turned toward them easily, unconcerned. "Officers—"

They hit him like a subway car, slamming his considerable bulk up against the wall and forcing him into a frisk position. He winced at the discomfort and then squeezed his head sideways so that he could glare straight into her flared eyes.

Guilt gnawed wildly. He hadn't actually hurt her. Or even tried to.

He simmered while they roughly frisked him up and down, relieving him of his phone and wallet and tossing them roughly to the ground. He stared at her the whole time, as though this was her fault and not his. But that molten gaze was even more unsettling close up and so she bent to retrieve his property and busied herself dusting them carefully off while the police pressed his face to the wall.

"What are you doing here?" one asked.

"Same thing you are. Checking on a jumper."

"That's our job, sir," the second cop volunteered as he finished searching the stranger's pockets.

The man looked back over his shoulder at the first officer, his hands still carefully pressed out to both sides. "Didn't look like it was going to happen before nightfall."

"Protocols," the first cop muttered tightly, a flush rushing up his thick neck.

They shoved him back into the wall for good measure and Tori winced on his behalf. Okay, this had gone far enough.

"Are you responsible for this?" The taller cop spoke before she could, leaning around to have a good look at the gaping entrance to her apartment where the door hung from just one ancient, struggling hinge. "This is damage to private property."

"Actually I think you'll find it's my property," the man gritted out.

All three faces swiveled back to him. "Excuse me?" the taller cop asked.

The man slowly turned, his hands still in clear view. "My name is Nathan Archer. I own this building." He nodded at the wallet that Tori still held. "My identification's in there."

All sympathy for him vanished between breaths. "*You're* our landlord?" She held his property out numbly.

One of the officers pulled the man's driver's license from the wallet and confirmed his identification. "This confirms your name but not your ownership of this building."

He looked at Tori. "Who do you pay rent to?"

A money-hungry, capitalist corporate shark. Tori narrowed her eyes. "Sanmore Holdings."

The stranger looked back at the cop holding his wallet. "Back compartment."

The cop pulled out a crisp white business card. "Nathan Archer, Chief Executive, Sanmore Holdings."

The cops immediately eased their hold on him and he straightened.

Nathan Archer. The man responsible for the state of her building. Probably living below fifty-ninth himself, and way too busy and important to worry about elevators not working or torn carpet under their feet. She played the only card she had left and pleaded to the rapidly-losing-interest police.

"It's still my door. I must have rights?"

The second cop looked her over lazily while his partner answered for him. "I guess you could get him for trespass."

Archer immediately transferred the full force of his glare

onto the second officer. Insanely, Tori missed the searing malevolence the moment it left her.

"Yes! Trespass. I didn't invite him in." She smiled triumphantly at her landlord for good measure.

That brought his eyes back to hers and her chest tightened up fractionally.

"I was saving your life."

She shoved her hands on her hips and stood her ground. "My life was just fine, thank you. I was fully rigged up."

"Not obvious from the street. Or from this side of the *locked* door," he added pointedly, his blue, blue eyes simmering but no longer furious. Not exactly. They flicked, lightning-fast, from her head to her toes and back again, and the simmer morphed into something a lot closer to interest—*sexual* interest. Breath clogged her throat as he blazed his intensity in her direction, every bit as naturally forceful as Niagara Falls.

In that moment the two cops ceased to exist.

It didn't help that a perky inner voice kept whispering over her shoulder, seducing her with reason, weaving amongst the subtle waves of his expensive scent and reminding her that he *had* been trying to help. She didn't want to be seduced by any part of this man. At all.

She wanted to be mad at him.

She straightened to her full height, shook off her conscience and spoke slowly, in case one of those thumps his head had taken at the hands of the local constabulary had dented his greedy, corporate brain. "You broke my door!"

"I'll buy you a new door," he said, calm and completely infuriating.

The police officers looked between them, bemused.

Tori glared up at him. "While you're buying stuff, how about a new washer for the ancient laundry? Or a door buzzer that works so we can quit calling messages up the stairwell."

The heat in his gaze swirled around her. He straightened and narrowed his eyes. "Nothing in this building is below code."

"Nothing in this building is particularly above it, either.

You do just enough to make sure you meet the tenancy act. We have heat and water and electrics that aren't falling out of the ceiling, but that's about it. The elevator doesn't even go all the way to the top floor."

"It never has."

"So that's a good enough reason not to fix it now? The woman in 12C is eighty years old. She shouldn't be hiking it up four flights of stairs. And the fire code—"

His eyes glittered. "The fire code specifies that you use the stairs in an emergency. They work fine. I know because I just ran up them to save your life!"

She stepped closer, her chest heaving and dragged her eyes off his lips. This close she could practically feel the furnace of his anger. "Not if you're an octogenarian!"

"Then she should take an apartment on one of the lower floors."

Tall as he was, he had to lean down toward her to get in her face. It caused a riot in her pulse. She lifted her chin and leaned toward him. "Those apartments are full of *other* old people—"

The shorter cop growled behind them. "Would you two like some privacy? Or maybe a room?"

Tori snapped around to look at the cop and then back to the man in front of her. Sure enough, she was standing dangerously close to Nathan Archer and the hallway fairly sparkled with the live current swirling around the two of them.

"I have a room," she grumbled to the officer, though her eyes stayed on the tallest man in the hallway. "I just don't have a door."

Archer's deep voice rumbled through tight lips. A rich man's lips. Though she did wonder what they would look like if he smiled.

"I'll have that fixed by dinnertime."

Too bad if she wanted to take a nap or...relax...or something before then! "So you do have a maintenance team at your disposal. You wouldn't know it from the general condition of the building—"

"There you go," one officer cut in loudly. "Complete restitution. I think we're done here."

She spun back to him. "We're not done. What about the trespass?" The officer looked apologetically at Archer.

Oh, please... "Seriously? One waft of a fancy business card and now the rich guy is calling the shots?"

All three of them looked at her as if she was mad. Pretty much where she imagined they'd started an hour ago, back when she was up the ledge. "I want him charged with trespass. He entered my apartment without my permission."

Archer tried again. "Come on. I was trying to save your life."

She tossed her hair back. "Tell that to the judge."

"I guess I'll have to."

One officer reluctantly took her details while the other spoke quietly to Archer a few meters down the hall. He smiled while the cop shook his head and chuckled.

She wedged her hands to her hips again and spoke loudly. "When you're completely done with the testosterone bonding..."

Her cop took a deep breath and turned to the taller man. "You have the right to remain silent. Anything you say..."

As the Miranda unfolded, Tori handed Archer his cell phone and tried hard not to meet his eyes. She had a way of losing focus when she did that. But her fingers touched his as he wrapped them around his BlackBerry and she flinched away from the intimate brush of skin on skin.

Her pulse stumbled.

"...if you cannot afford an attorney..."

As if. He probably surrounded himself with attorneys. His fine white business shirt looked like it cost more than he spent on this building in a year.

The cops walked Archer back toward the stairs, finishing up their legal responsibilities. At some point someone decided handcuffs were overkill—*shame*—but Archer limped obediently between them anyway, speaking quietly into his phone and only half listening as his rights were fully enumerated.

As the cops sandwiched him through the door to the stairwell, he glanced back at her, a lock of dark hair falling across his forehead between those Hollywood eyes. He didn't look the slightest bit disturbed by the threat of legal action. For some reason, that only made her madder.

How often did this guy get arrested?

"Better save that single phone call they'll give you in lock-up," she yelled down the hall to them. "You're going to need it to call someone about my door!"

CHAPTER TWO

"YOUR Honor—"

"Save it, Mr. Archer," the judge said, "I've made my ruling. I recognise that you meant well in going to the assistance of the plaintiff, however, the fact remains that you broke into her apartment and did material damage to her door and lock—"

"Which I fixed…"

The judge raised one hand and silenced him. "And that even though it was technically your own property, Ms Morfitt is afforded some protection under New York's Tenancy Protection Act, which makes her suit of trespass reasonable."

"If petty," Nate murmured. His attorney, business partner and best friend, Dean, counseled him to hold his tongue. Probably just as well or he'd end up behind bars for contempt. This whole thing was a ridiculous waste of his time—time that could have been better spent at his desk earning a bunch of zeroes for his company. All over a broken door that had been fixed the same day. If all his building's tenants were from the same planet as Viktoria Morfitt he'd be happy to see the back of them when he developed the site.

"I was trying to help her," he said flatly, for the hundredth time. No one but him seemed to care.

"Your file indicates that you specialize in Information Technology, is that correct?" the judge asked. She said that as though he was some kind of help-desk operator instead of the founder of one of the most successful young IT companies on the east coast.

Dean spoke just as Nate was about to educate her. "That is correct, Your Honor."

The judge didn't take her eyes off Nate's. Thinking. Plotting. "I'm going to commute your sentence, Mr. Archer, so that it doesn't haunt your record for the rest of your life. One hundred hours of community service to be undertaken within thirty days."

"Community service? Do you know what one hundred hours of my time *costs*?"

Dean swooped in to stop him saying more. "My client would be willing to pay financial compensation in lieu, Your Honor."

Willing was a stretch but he'd go with it.

The judge looked at Nate archly, and he stared solidly back at her. Then she dragged her eyes to his left. "No doubt, Counselor, but that's not on the table. The purpose of a service order is to give the defendant time to reflect. To learn. Not to make it all go away with the sweep of their assistant's pen." Nate could practically feel the order doubling in length. Or severity. She made some notes on the documentation in front of her, eyes narrowed. "Mr. Archer, I'm going to recommend you undertake your service on behalf of the plaintiff."

His stomach lurched. *Note to self: never upset a district judge.* "Are you serious?"

"Nate—" Dean just about choked in his haste to silence him, but then changed tack as the judge leaned as far forward as she could possibly go without tumbling from her lofty perch. "Thank you, Your Honor. We'll see that it happens."

But Nate spread his hands wide and tried one more time. "I was trying to help her, judge."

Dean's hand slid onto his forearm and gripped it hard. The judge's lips drew even tighter. "Which is why it's not a two-hundred-hour order, Mr. Archer. Counselor, please explain to your client that this is a judicial sentence, not a Wall Street negotiation."

Nate ignored that. "But what will I do for her?"

"Help her with her laundry? I really don't care. My order is set." She eyed the man by Nate's side. "Is that clear, Counselor?"

"It is, Your Honor, thank you." Dean whispered furiously in Nate's ear that a commuted service order was as good as invisible on his record.

"Easy for you to say," Nate growled. "That's not one hundred hours of *your* executive time." Spent in a building he preferred not to even think about.

The judge with super hearing lifted one arch brow. "I think you'll find that my time is just as valuable as yours, Mr. Archer, and you've taken up quite enough of it. Next!"

The gavel came down on any hope of someone seeing reason in all this lunacy.

Ten minutes later it was all over; Nate and Dean trod down the marble stairs of the justice building and shook hands. From an attorney's perspective it was a good outcome, but the idea of not only spending time in that building—with *her*…

Viktoria Morfitt's suit for trespass was ridiculous and everyone knew it. The cops. The judge. Even the woman herself, judging by the delicate little lines that had formed between her brows as the cops had escorted him from his own building.

But he'd spooked her out on the ledge and then made the tactical error of letting her know he was her landlord. If he'd kept his trap shut she probably would have let him off with the promise of restitution for the door. But no…He'd played the rare *do-you-know-who-I-am?* card, and she'd taken her first opportunity to let him know exactly what she thought about his building management.

Not very much.

And now he had a hundred hours of community service to think about how he might have done things differently.

"There's a morning we'll never get back," Dean grumbled

comfortably. "But don't worry about it, I'll get appeal paperwork straight off. Though you might have to do a few hours before that gets processed."

"When am I supposed to start this farce?"

"The judge's decree will be lodged after two-thirty today, but, reasonably, tomorrow will be fine. That'll give the public defender time to alert your jumper to the order."

"I'm sure she'll be thrilled."

"I'm sure she won't," his friend said, turning and trotting down the steps with a chuckle. "But the Archer charm hasn't failed you yet."

The fact that was true didn't really make things any better. One hundred hours with a human porcupine in a building he could barely stomach.

Great.

Tori filled her lungs behind her brand-new door and composed herself. The judge must have been having a badly hormonal day to task someone like Nathan Archer with community service. Either that or his smug confidence had got up Her Honor's nose as much as it had irritated *her* last week. Not hard to imagine.

Now or never… She pulled the door nice and wide and made a show of leaning on it. Showcasing it. "Mr. Archer."

The breath closest to her lips froze in its tracks at the sight of him filling her doorway and all her other breaths jammed up behind it in an oxygen pile-up.

Fortunately, he didn't notice as his blue eyes examined the door critically. "Could they have found anything less suitable?"

She looked at the modern, perfect door which was so out of place in a 1901 building. "I assumed you picked it specifically. But it locks, so I'm happy."

She'd forgotten how those eyes *really* felt when they rested on her. Like twin embers from a fire alighting on her skin.

Warm at first touch, but smoldering to an uncomfortable burn the longer they lingered.

"Well, one of us is, at least," he mumbled.

She couldn't stop the irritated sigh that escaped her. "I didn't ask for this community service, Mr. Archer. I'm no more thrilled than you are." The last thing she wanted was to be forced into the company of such a disagreeable stranger, with the uncomfortable responsibility of tasking him with chores.

Silence fell, and the only sound to interrupt it was 10A's television blaring out late afternoon *Sesame Street*.

He stared at her until finally saying, "May I come in?"

Heat broiled just below her collar. Leaving him standing in the hall… She stood back and let all six-foot-three of him into her home. "So how does this work?"

He shrugged those massive shoulders. "Search me, this is my first offence."

Tori winced, knowing that—truthfully—he'd done nothing more than try to help her. But one hundred hours was a small price to pay for how he'd neglected the building they both stood in. "Hey, service orders are the latest celebrity accessory. You can't buy that kind of street cred."

He turned and shot her a dark look from under perfectly manicured brows. Every glare he used was a glare wasted. She really didn't care whether or not he was happy. He was only her landlord.

She took his coat and turned to hang it on the back of her front door before remembering her new one didn't have a hook. She detoured via the sofa to drape it over the back. The contrast between the expensive fabric of his coat and the aged upholstery of her sofa couldn't have been more marked.

"Something's been bothering me," he said, turning those blue eyes on her. "About last week."

Only one thing? Quite a lot had been bothering her about it. Her reaction to his closeness not the least.

"What were you doing out on that ledge?" he continued.

"Not jumping."

"So I gathered."

She stared at him and then crossed to the large photo album on the coffee table. She spun it in his direction and flipped it open. "These are Wilma and Fred."

He leaned down to look at the range of photographs artfully displayed on the page. "Hawks?"

"Peregrine falcons. They live wild in this area."

Deep blue eyes lifted to hers. "And…?"

"And I was installing a nest box for them."

He blinked at her. "Out on the ledge?"

She clenched her teeth to avoid rolling her eyes. "I tried it in here, but it just didn't do as well." *Idiot.*

Archer grunted and Tori's arms stole round her midsection while he flicked through the various images in her album.

"These are good," he finally said. "Who took them?"

"I did."

His head came up. "Where from?"

She pulled back the breezy curtain from her living-room window to reveal spotless glass. "There's another window in the bedroom. Sometimes I use the roof. Mostly the ledge."

"So that wasn't your first dangerous foray out there?"

"It's not dangerous. I'm tethered at all times."

He lifted aristocratic eyebrows. "To a century-old building?"

A century-old building that's crumbling around you. He might as well have said it. It was perfectly evident to anyone who cared to look. The neglect wouldn't fly in Morningside proper, but being right on the border of West Harlem, he was getting away with it. Of course he was. Money talked around here.

"I pick the strongest point I can to fix to," she said.

He looked at the pictures again. "You must have some great equipment."

She shrugged. Let him believe that it was the camera that took the photo, not the person behind it. "I've always enjoyed wildlife photography." More than just enjoyed. She'd been on track to make a career out of it back when she'd graduated.

He reached the back pages of the album. "These ones weren't taken out your window." He flipped it her way and her heart gave a little lurch. An aerie with a stunning mountain vista stretching out in all directions behind it. An eagle in flight, its full wings spread three meters wide. Both taken from high points.

Really, *really* high points.

"I took those in the Appalachians and Cascades," she said, tightly, but then she forced the topic back to her city peregrines before he could ask any more questions. As far as she knew, this court order didn't come with the requirement for full disclosure about her past.

"Fred and Wilma turned up in our skies about three months ago, and then about four weeks ago they started visiting this building more and more. I made them a nest box for the coming breeding season so they don't have to perch precariously on a transformer or bridge or something."

So she could have a little bit of her old life here in her new one.

"Hawks..." He closed the album carefully and placed it gently back on the coffee table. Then he stood there not saying a word. Just thinking.

"So..." She cleared her throat. "Should we talk about how this is going to work? What you can do here for one hundred hours?"

His eyes bored into her and triggered a temperature spike. "I sense you've been giving it some thought?"

She crossed to the kitchen and took up the sheet of notepaper she'd prepared. "I made a list."

His lips twisted. "Really—of what?"

"Of all the things wrong with the building. Things that you can fix in one hundred hours."

The laundry. The elevator. The floors. The buzzer...

His eyebrows rose as he read down the page. "Long list."

"It's a bad building."

His long lashes practically obscured his eyes, they narrowed so far. "So why do you live here?"

Her stomach shriveled into a prune under his scrutiny. "Because I can afford it. Because it's close to the parks." Not that she'd visited those in a long time. But it was why she'd chosen this building originally.

He continued reading the list. "Just one problem."

"Why did I know there'd be a 'just'?"

He ignored her. "The judge's decree is firm on me not outsourcing any of this service. It has to be by my own hand. Most of this list calls for tradesmen."

She stared at him. "It hadn't occurred to me that you'd actually follow the order. You struck me as a corner-cutter."

"Not at all."

She matched his glare. "The front-door buzzer's still faulty."

"That's not about cutting corners—*or costs*," he said just as she was about to accuse him of precisely that.

"What is it, then?"

He folded his arms across his chest, highlighting its vast breadth. "It's asset strategy."

Her snort was unladylike in the extreme. "Is your strategy to let the building and everyone in it crumble to dust? If so, then you're right on target."

Was that the tiniest hint of color at his collar? He laid the list down on the table. "I've accepted the terms of the order. I'll see it through. My way."

"So what can you do? What *do* you do?"

His grunt was immediate. "I do a lot of paperwork. I sign things. Spend money."

"Just not here."

He ignored that. "I'm in the information industry."

Tori threw her hands up. "Well, what's that going to be useful for?"

It took the flare of his pupils to remind her how offensive

he might find that. And then she wondered why she cared all about offending him. "I mean, here…in my apartment."

"Actually, I have an idea. It relates to your birds."

"The falcons?"

"Urban raptors are a big deal on Manhattan. There are a number of webcams set up across the city, beaming out live images to the rest of the world. Kind of a virtual ecotourism. For those who are interested."

The way he said it made it perfectly clear of how little interest they were to him.

"I guess. I was just doing it for me." And in some ways she'd enjoyed keeping the peregrine falcon pair a special thing. A private thing. Which was probably selfish. The whole world should be able to see the beauty of nature. Wasn't that what her photography was all about? "A webcam, you think?"

"And a website. One's pointless without the other."

Flutters fizzed up inside her like champagne and the strangeness of it only made her realize how long it had been since something had really excited her. A website full of her images, full of her beautiful birds. For everyone to see. She knew about the other falcon locations in New York but hadn't thought for a moment she might ever be able to do something similar in Morningside.

"You can design a website?"

His expression darkened. "Sanmore's mailboy can design a simple website. As can half the fifth graders on Manhattan. It's no big deal."

Not for him, maybe. She turned her mind to the ledge. "I guess it wouldn't be too hard to set a camera up on the ledge, focused on the nest box. If anything of interest happens, it'll probably happen there."

"How can you be sure they'll use the box?" he asked.

"I can't. But I'm encouraging them down every day. So I'm optimistic."

His eyes narrowed. "Encouraging?"

Might as well tell it as it was. "Luring. They're usually

pigeon eaters, but mice are easier to trap. This building has no shortage."

His lips thinned. "All buildings have vermin."

Her laugh was raw. "Not this many."

He stared at her, considering. "Excuse me a moment." Then he stepped into her small kitchen and spoke in quiet tones into the cell phone she'd held for him the week before. When he returned, his expression was impassive. "You may need to find a new source of bird bait."

She frowned. "What did you just do?"

"I took care of the vermin problem."

"With one phone call?"

"I have good staff."

One phone call. It could have been solved so long before this. "Good staff but not residential agents, I'd say. We've been reporting the mice for eighteen months."

He thought about that. "I trust our agent to take care of code issues."

"This is the same agent you trusted with my door selection?"

His eyes shifted back to the hideously inappropriate door and she felt a mini rush of satisfaction that she'd finally scored a point. But snarking at him wasn't going to be a fun way to spend the next hundred hours. And as much as she'd like to make him suffer just a little bit for the torn carpet and clunky pipes and glacially slow elevator, she had to endure it, too. And she had a feeling he would give as good as he got.

"Anyway," she said. "I'm sure raw meat will suffice in the unlikely event I run out of fresh food."

"Then what? They'll just…come?"

She slid her hands onto her hips. "Is this interest? Or are you just being polite?"

His left eye twitched slightly. "I have a court order that says I should be interested, Ms. Morfitt. No offense."

She arched a single eyebrow. People like him had no idea how offensive their very existence was to people like her. To every tenant who scraped together the rent to live in his shabby building. To the people who went without every day so he could have another sportscar in his parking space.

Her birds had no way of making him money; therefore, they didn't rate for Nathan Archer.

"None taken." She wouldn't give him the satisfaction. "I'm planning on moving the mice to the nest box tomorrow, to see how the falcons respond to it."

"Might as well get the camera set up and operating straightaway, then," he said.

"You're assuming I've agreed?"

"Haven't you? Your eyes twinkled like the Manhattan skyline when I suggested it."

It burned her that he could read her so easily. And it bothered her that he was paying that much attention to what her eyes were doing. Bothered and…something else. Her chest pressed in tighter.

She shook the rogue thought loose. "Can we use something small and unobtrusive? I don't want to scare them away just as they're starting to come close. It took me weeks to get them accustomed to visiting the ledge, and any day now they'll need to start laying."

He moved to the window and looked out, examining the wall material. "I can probably core out one of the stone blocks in the basement and fit the camera into it. They'll barely know it's there."

She smiled. "There you go, then. You're not totally without practical skills."

He opened his mouth to argue, but then seemed to think better of it. "I'll need your bathroom."

She flinched. That seemed a stupidly unsettling and intimate request—not that the dictatorial words in any way resembled a request. The man was going to be here for one hundred hours—of course he was going to need the facilities at some point.

She stepped back from the doorway. "You know the way."

One brow twitched. "You're not coming?"

Both her own shot upward. "Uh...no, you'll have to manage by yourself." Who knew, maybe the man had assistants for that, too.

"You're going to play hardball on this court order, aren't you? Well, don't come crying to me if I pull out something I shouldn't."

What? Tori frowned after his retreating figure. Then, as she heard the exaggerated *ziiip,* her frown doubled and she muttered, "What, Mr. Corporate America isn't a door-closer?"

Seconds later she heard another metallic *ziiip* and she realized her mistake. Heat flared up her throat. The man wasn't peeing. He was measuring—with a steel tape measure. Probably the ledge window.

Of course he was.

And she'd just come across as the biggest moron ever to breathe. Things were off to a great start.

Just fabulous.

Nathan turned out of West 126th Street onto St. Nicholas Avenue and wove his way through the late-afternoon pedestrian traffic heading for the subway. It didn't matter that it was nearly evening—activity levels at nearby Columbia University didn't drop until much later, which meant the streets around it were perpetually busy during class hours. Even a few blocks away. He'd spent a lot of time out on these streets as a kid—more than most—so he knew every square inch.

Something about Tori Morfitt really got his people antennae twitching. What was a young, beautiful woman—a wildlife photographer—doing living alone in his shabby building, with no job or family that he could discern, spending her time hanging out with birds?

In a world where he tended to attract compliant yes-men—and *oh-yes* women—encountering someone so wholly unconcerned about appropriateness, someone who wore their heart so dangerously on their sleeve was a refreshing change. When she forgot to be angry with him she was quite easygoing: bright, sharp, compassionate. And the immediate blaze of her eyes as he'd suggested the webcam had reached out, snared him by the intestines and slowly reeled him in.

No doubt his interest would waver the moment he uncovered her mysteries, but for now… There were worse ways of spending time—and community service—than with a lithe, healthy young woman who liked to spar verbally.

He pulled out his phone as he walked.

"Dean," he said the moment his attorney answered his call.

"Hey, Nate."

"Forget the appeal, will you?"

"Are you serious?" He could almost hear the frown in his friend's voice—a full two-eyebrow job. What he was really asking was, *Are you insane*? "I can get you off."

"I'd rather see it out, Dean. It's a principle thing."

"You sure you can afford the moral high ground right now? We have a lot on."

His friend's gentle censure merged with the noise of the traffic. "I'll fit everything in. You know that. It's been a long time since I had anyone to get home to." He jogged between cars across the street and joined the salmon-spawn crush on the subway stairs. "Who's going to care if I pull some late ones at the office?"

"You're superhuman, Nate, not invincible."

"I don't want to lawyer my way out of this. Call it strategy—a good chance to get a handle on the lay of the land at Morningside, tenant-wise."

A good chance to get a handle on one particular tenant, at least.

Dean took his time answering. "Wow. She must be something."

Nate instantly started feeling tetchy. If he had to face an inquisition he might as well go back to Tori's. "Who?"

"Your jumper."

"She wasn't jumping."

"Don't change the subject. This is about her, isn't it?"

Nate surged forward as he saw the subway car preparing to move off. "This is about me remembering where I came from. How things were done before the money."

Dean sobered immediately. "The building's getting to you, huh?"

Nate shouldered his way between closing subway doors and leaned on the glass partition. "I just don't want to buy my way out of this."

"So you keep saying. But I'm not convinced. You worked hard all your life precisely so that you could have access to the freedom money buys."

"Yeah, but I'll do my hundred hours and then walk away knowing I did it the right way." Knowing that *she* knew it.

Dean thought about that. "Your call, buddy."

"Thank you. You can withdraw the appeal?"

"Consider it done."

Nate signed off and slid his phone back into his pocket.

One hundred hours with Tori Morfitt and he got to keep the moral high ground. A win-win. His favorite type of outcome.

He had some guilt about the effort they were about to go to in setting up the webcam but, at the end of the day, it was his effort to waste. He'd be doing most of the work. And it wouldn't be totally pointless. His plans to redevelop the building site wouldn't kick off for months so they'd get one good season out of the webcam, at least.

Of course, it meant spending more hours in the building where he was born than he particularly wanted to, but he'd control that. He'd managed the feelings his whole childhood, how hard could it be now? Memories started to morph from the gray haze he usually maintained into more concrete shapes and sounds.

He went for his phone again and dialed his office rather than let them take root in his consciousness.

"Karin, I'm heading back. What have I missed?"

As always, work did a sensational job of shoving the

memories to one side. It had served him well for fifteen years and it didn't fail him now as the subway rattled him back down-town to his own world.

CHAPTER THREE

"ARE you sure this is safe?"

Twenty-four hours later, Nathan was hanging out Tori's window again, watching her fit the stone block he'd brought with him into the corner of the ledge opposite the nest box. It was artfully hollowed out, and comfortably housed a small black camera, the lens poking discreetly out the front. The peregrines would notice nothing unusual when they returned after an evening's hunting and the camera would be protected from New York's wilder weather.

"It's safe. I've been much higher than this," Tori said through tight lips, not because she was frightened, but because she didn't like to talk about climbing. Sometimes she didn't even like to *think* about climbing. It made her feel things she was better off suppressing. She shifted her weight, wedged her scaling boot more firmly in the corner, and slid the block fully back into position.

"Better you than me," he murmured.

"Not good with heights?" she teased lightly.

"I love heights. My company's forty floors up. It's falling to my death I'm not so wild about."

Tori's body responded instantly to his words, locking up hard, squeezing her lungs so hard they couldn't inflate. It took all her concentration to will them open again so that air could rush in. She faked busy work with the camera to buy a couple of recovery seconds.

When she could speak again, she said, "You seemed ready enough to lurch out here last week."

"I thought you were in trouble. I wasn't really thinking about myself."

Sure. And hell had an ice-hockey team. Her money was on him thinking very much about the bad publicity that goes with a jumper. She turned and gathered up some of the scattered substrate from the nesting box and returned it to where it could do the birds more good.

"Won't it all just blow out again?" he asked, watching her clean-up effort. "It's gusty up here."

"It's heavier than it looks, so it doesn't blow. The peregrines toss it all out while investigating the box. They'll probably just do it again but at least it will have started fully set up for their needs. It's all I can do. They seem to like it this way."

He shrugged and mumbled, "The hawk wants what the hawk wants."

Curiosity drew her gaze back to him. So he did have a sense of humor, albeit a reluctant one. "Well, if they'd *want* a little more tidily that would be great for me." She sat back on her haunches and examined the now-tidy box, then looked at the hidden camera. A thrill of excitement raced up her spine. Nothing like the adrenaline dump of her climbing days, but it was something. "Okay. I think we're done."

She scooted backwards and twisted through the window, taking care not to snag the new cable that draped through it, connecting the camera to the small temporary monitor set up in her bathroom. Nathan stood back and let her back in.

"When I come next I'll hook it up to your TV so you can watch it with the flick of a switch," he said, shifting his focus politely from the midriff she exposed as her T-shirt snagged on the window latch.

"If I have a couple of nesting peregrines to watch, I'm not going to be switching anywhere," she said. Having the nest visible via closed circuit television would be a vast improvement on leaning out her window every day. Less likely to disturb the birds, too.

She lifted her gaze to him as she stepped down off the toilet seat and killed her height advantage. "That would be great, thank you."

Neither of them moved from the cramped bathroom, but Archer clearly had no more idea what to do with genuine gratitude from her than she did. A tiny crease marred the perfectly groomed place between his eyebrows. Her breathing picked up pace as she stared up at him, and her lips fell open slightly. His sharp eyes followed every move. Then his own parted and Tori's breath caught.

A rapid tattoo on the door snapped them both from the awkward place where silent seconds had just passed. A subtle rush of disappointment abseiled through her veins. Her face turned toward her new front door and then the rest of her followed, almost reluctantly. "That will be Mr. Broswolowski."

She squeezed past Nate's body carefully, failing at total clearance, and twisted slightly to avoid rudely shouldering him in the chest. That only served to brush her front against him as she moved through into the living room. If she'd been stacked instead of athletic it would have been totally gratuitous. As it was, his tight jaw barely shifted and his eyes only flicked briefly downwards.

While her breath tightened unaccountably.

She flung the front door wide as soon as she got to it.

"Aren't you the Queen of Sheba," the elderly man standing in the hall said as he admired her spotless new door. "Need to get yourself a peephole, though. This isn't the upper west side, you know."

Tori laughed as he entered. "I knew you by your knock, Mr. Broswolowski."

The man dumped a large hamper of clean laundry on her coffee table and commenced his standard grumble. "This basket doesn't get any lighter coming up two flights of stairs. What use is an elevator if it can't go to all floors?" He straightened uncomfortably.

"I keep telling you to bring them to me dirty. I can launder them for you before I iron them. Save your spine."

"I'm not so old that I'm prepared to have a pretty girl go through my dirty linens. The stairs are fine. But that washer isn't getting any more efficient."

Nathan chose that moment to fully emerge from the direction of the bathroom. Mr. Broswolowski looked up then turned in surprise to Tori.

"Mr. Broswolowski, this is—" for no good reason she hesitated to sic her acerbic downstairs neighbor on their landlord "—a friend of mine. He's helping me with the falcons."

"Is that so?"

Tori held her breath and waited for the awkward comment to come; some observation to the effect that her neighbor had never seen her with a man, let alone had one wander out of her bathroom as if he owned the place. Which, of course, he did. Not that she was going to share the fact. *Her* giving Nathan Archer grief was one thing, but exposing him to the collective grizzles of all her neighbors…

"Just the usual, Mr. B?"

The older man might struggle with his eyes and his arthritis, but his mind was in perfect working order. He let his curiosity dissipate, which was uncharacteristic; heavy hints usually only spurred him on. But he glanced more than once at Nathan's imposing figure and Tori realized this was the first time she'd seen Mr. B outgunned.

"Bless you, yes. There's a few more than usual," he said. "I'm spring-cleaning."

She nudged him toward the door. "Cranes or peacocks?"

He let himself be bundled out into the hall. "In a hurry, Tori?"

"Time is money, Mr. B."

"Like either of us needs to worry about time." He chuckled, before adding, "Peacocks."

Tori returned his smile. He was so predictable. "Done. I'll have them to you by tomorrow afternoon."

"Yes, yes. I wouldn't want to interrupt your date..."

She clicked the door shut behind them pointedly as she followed the older man into the hall, to lessen the chance of Nathan hearing. "It's not a date. It's business."

"*Some* kind of business, anyway," Mr. B mumbled, turning away happily.

"None of yours, that's for sure," she called after him. His laugh ricocheted back towards her down the dim hallway. She turned and pushed the door to go back in, but it didn't budge. Her lashes fell closed. That's right...new door.

New *self-locking* door.

She took a deep breath and knocked, steeling herself for the inevitable questions. If she got lucky, Nathan would have gone back to work on the camera and not heard a word Mr. B had said. If she got lucky he'd not be the slightest bit interested in what she and her neighbors got up to.

But it had been a long time since she considered herself lucky

An old sorrow sliced through her.

"Come in," Nathan said with a satisfied mouth-twist as he opened her door. His eyes travelled to the basket overflowing with linens still sitting on the coffee table. "You do his laundry?"

She shifted the clean linen over to the service cupboard that served as a closet and lifted her chin. "He has arthritis. Ironing hurts him."

The frown deepened. "What was with the peacock?"

Awkwardness leached through her. Speaking of *none of your business...* But his question seemed genuine enough. To an outsider it probably did seem crazy. "I like to make it special. Fun. I do a sort of hot-steam origami with his linen. He likes the peacock fan for his sheets."

"Doesn't that defeat the purpose of ironing?"

She smiled. "He doesn't seem to mind. I did it one Christmas as a surprise and it's kind of…stuck."

"*One* Christmas? How long have you been doing it?"

She frowned. Wow. Had it really been four years? "A while."

"Does he pay you?"

Heat surged. Was everything about money for him? "Worried I'm operating a home business without a license?"

"No," he said. "Just curious."

He shoved his hands into deep pockets, lifting the hem of his expensive coat and flashing the line of his dark leather belt where a crisp white shirt tucked neatly into a narrow waist. It had been a long time since she'd been this close to someone in formal business wear. And a long time since she'd seen someone whom business wear suited quite so much. She immediately thought of her brother dressed up to the nines on his first day at his first Portland job. He'd been so overly pressed and so excited.

Her chest tightened. A lifetime ago.

"We have a kind of barter system going. Mr. Broswolowski was a stage producer and he's still got connections."

"You're an actor?"

Her laugh then was immediate. The idea of her standing on stage in front of hundreds of strangers… Her stomach knotted just from the image. "No. But Angel on three is, and Mr. Broswolowski throws her opportunities every now and again in return for me doing his laundry."

"Wait… You do his laundry and someone else reaps the benefit?"

"I benefit. Angel babysits the deCosta boy half a day a week as a thank you for Mr. B's inside information, and in return Mrs. deCosta brings me fresh groceries every Monday when she does her own run."

If he frowned any more his forehead was going to split down the middle. "Just how many people are involved in this scheme?" he asked.

"Across the whole building? Pretty much everyone, one way or another."

He gaped. "Thirty-six households?"

"Thirty-five. 8B's been empty for years. But pretty much everyone else gets involved in one way or another. It suits our needs. And it's economical. Doing Mr. B's ironing keeps my refrigerator stocked."

"What happens when the deCosta boy gets too old for babysitting?"

Tori blinked. Straight to the weak link in the supply chain. No wonder he was a squillionaire. "Laundry's not my only trade. I have other assets."

His laugh was more of a grunt. "A regular domestic portfolio."

She fought the prickles that begged to rise. "Hey, I didn't start it. Some poor kid with an entrepreneurial spirit came up with it in the eighties as a way of making ends meet. But it works for me."

Inexplicably his whole face tightened. His voice grew tight. "You do know you can have groceries delivered to your door?"

Tori blinked at him. "Sure. But who would do Mr. B's ironing?"

The Captain of Industry seemed to have no good answer for that. He stared at her, long and hard. "I guess you have a point."

She fought down her instinctive defensiveness. The man was just trying to make conversation. "It's not like it's against the law, it's just neighbors getting together to help each other out."

He turned back on a judgmental eyebrow-lift. "You're exchanging services for gratuities."

Heat blazed. "I do someone's *ironing.* You make it sound like I'm selling sexual favours in the hallway. That hasn't happened in this building for a decade."

He spun toward the television, but not before she saw the

way his face rapidly dumped its color. All of it. Every part of her wanted to apologise, but…what for? *He'd* insulted *her.*

She sighed. "How about we just stick to what we're here for." She took a deep breath. "Tell me about this CCTV jig."

He took a moment before emerging from behind her modest television. "This doesn't have the inputs I need. I'll bring you a new one."

"A new what?"

"A new television."

"You will not!"

He blinked at her. "This one won't work with the CCTV gear."

"I'm not accepting a gift like that from you to get you out of community service."

His eyes narrowed. "Have I asked you to let me off the service order?"

"I'm sure you're working up to it." She lifted her chin and absorbed the tiny adrenaline rush that came with sparring with him.

"You really don't have a very high opinion of me, do you?"

Tori frowned. "I've been entrusted with…I feel like there's an obligation there."

"To do what?"

"To sign your attendance. Properly."

"Like some kind of classroom roll call?" The stare he gave her went on forever. "And you wouldn't consider just signing it off to be rid of me?"

Oh, how she'd love to be rid of him. Except someone had forgotten to tell her skin that. The way it tingled when she opened the door to him this afternoon… The way it prickled even now, under his glare.

She shrugged. "They're trusting me."

"You don't know them."

"It doesn't matter. *I* would know."

"Well if you want me to do this by the book you're going

to need to take the television, otherwise there can be no webcam."

"I can't accept a television."

"Ms Morfitt—"

"Oh, for crying out loud, will you call me Viktoria? Or Tori. You make me feel like an aging spinster." And that likelihood was something she tried very hard not to think about. Living it later was going to be hard enough…

She stood and moved toward the kitchen. Toward her ever-bubbling coffeepot.

"Viktoria…"

Nathan frowned, not liking the formal sound of it on his lips and tried again as she moved away from him. "Tori. I run an IT empire; we have monitors and televisions littering my office. Giving you one is about as meaningful to me as giving you corporate stationery."

Her nostrils flared and he felt like a schmuck. She'd done the very best she could with the bare bones of this apartment but there was no disguising the absence of money in her world. Not surprising if she was living on a barter system. And here he was throwing around televisions as if they were nothing. Which—brutal truth be told—they were, in his world. But waving his worth around wasn't usually his style. Money had come hard to him, but he wasn't so far gone he forgot what it felt like to live the other way.

One minute back in this building and it was all too fresh. Uncomfortably so.

"Look. You'll need it to monitor the web feed. I need it to get this community service order signed off." She looked entirely unmoved. He searched around for inspiration.

It wasn't hard for him to get into the trading spirit. That junior entrepreneur she spoke of living in the building twenty years ago had been *him*. He'd had a raft of creative schemes going to try and make something from the nothing of his youth. Not that he was going to tell her that. "I'll trade you if I have to."

Her gray eyes scanned his body critically and a tingle of honeyed warmth trailed everywhere she looked. He'd never been more grateful that he kept in good shape under the designer suits. Which was ludicrous—just because *she* was in perfect shape. The way she'd twisted in through that window—

His whole body twitched.

"You don't look like someone who needs their ironing done," she said, carefully. "What am I going to trade you for?"

The spark of defiance and pride in her expression touched him somewhere down deep. Enough to ask her seriously, "What can you offer me?"

She frowned. "Photography?"

As good as her images were, did she truly think she had nothing else to offer? He wanted to push her. To show her otherwise. A good brain ticked away beneath those tumbling auburn locks. Never mind the fact this was a great chance to learn a little more about her. "I don't need it. I have a whole marketing department for that stuff."

Her delicate brows dipped. "Well…if we're talking something you *need*…"

Crap. He should have taken the photography.

"…how about I show you around your building?" she continued. "Introduce you to people. Show you the human face of this towering *asset*."

Nate's heart doubled in size and pressed hard against his lungs. Despite what he'd told Dean, getting to know his tenants was the last thing he wanted. Not when he was about to rip the building out from under them. But it did mean Tori would take the new television and that meant he'd get his life back ninety-five hours from now. And as a side bonus, he could get to know her better.

"Not that I can see how that actually benefits me, but I accept." Whatever it took. He'd just stall her indefinitely on her part of the bargain.

"Of course it benefits you. I'm sure you know your tenants

are an asset too. Some of them have lived here all their lives. You don't get more loyal customers than that."

...all their lives.

That meant some of them might have lived here back when *he* lived here. And when *she* lived here. His mother. Nate's skin tingled. Meeting those tenants was definitely out of the question. And therefore getting chummy with the natives was categorically not on his radar.

Except maybe this one. Surly or not, Tori grabbed his attention in a way no other woman had. A two-handed grab.

"I'll have the television delivered tomorrow," he cut in, shaking the image free. "Will you be home?"

"Yep."

"I haven't given you a time yet."

She shrugged. "I'll be home. I have a date with a *Battlestar Galactica* marathon and Mr. B's ironing, remember?"

For some reason, the thought of the same hands that took such artistic wildlife photos sweltering behind a steam iron all day made him uncomfortable. But what Viktoria Morfitt chose to do with her spare time was entirely her own business.

And her business was none of his business.

"Tori Morfitt, door!"

A man in a hemp beanie flung the front door wide and let Nate into the ground floor of his own building the next day, then hollered Tori's name up the stairwell. Somewhere upstairs, someone else echoed the call. And then someone else as the message passed up the building frontier-style.

"Buzzer doesn't work," the man finally said by way of awkward conversation and then turned back to scanning his mail.

Nate's smile was tight. What could he say? That was *his* buzzer doing such a bad job of providing security for his tenants. Fortunately, the neighbors had it covered—this guy wasn't letting him go anywhere until Tori appeared and vouched for him.

Security by proxy.

"She's jogging so she shouldn't be long," the guy eventually said, taking an exaggerated amount of time sorting through his post. Nate turned and looked outside, confused. He hadn't passed her in the street… Then again, Morningside was a campus district, full of people at all hours, and she might prefer the ease of the public parks. He turned more fully to watch the path that led up from the sidewalk to the foyer door.

Anyone would think he was looking forward to it.

The stairwell door burst open behind him, snapping his head back around. Tori came through flushed, sweating and kitted out in tight running gear. Her eyes flared as they hit him and she stumbled to a halt. "You're early."

Her chest rose and fell heavily with each breath. He concentrated extra hard on keeping his focus high, but it wasn't easy, given her training top was more bandage than clothing and her skin glistened with sweat along her breast line. "I had a meeting in Jersey. I figured there was no point going back downtown for only half an hour."

He took in the way she ran her palms down her tight-fitting workout gear. She looked as though she wanted to be anywhere else than here—with him. "Sorry. Is it a problem?"

"No. I just…" She pushed her fingers through damp hair. "Come on up."

As they turned, she threw a smile at beanie guy. "Thanks, Danny."

Danny gave her a keen smile and Nate immediately stood straighter as a surge of territoriality hit him out of nowhere. *Ridiculous.* As if she'd go for the half-washed hippie type anyway.

As he headed for the elevator, he realized he had no idea what type of guy she did go for. Not his type, judging by how quickly she took offense at just about everything he did.

"You're taking the stairs?" he said as she let him enter the elevator alone.

"I'll meet you up there," she said. "I'm nearly done with

my workout. And you really don't want to be locked in a small space with me right now. The rate that elevator moves I might even get there before you."

She turned and disappeared back through the door, leaving Nate to enter the elevator alone. As it happened, he couldn't think of anything better than being closed in a small space with Tori Morfitt—sweat or no sweat. Something about standing so close to all that radiating heat while he was buttoned up in his best three-piece… His subconscious slapped him for the pleasurable twinge that flicked through him, low and sharp.

She hadn't meant to get caught out in Lycra, all hot and bothered.

He pulled out his phone the moment the old doors slid shut and—as he had every time he got into this elevator—he picked a spot of carpet to focus on and kept his eyes glued there rather than look at himself in the age-speckled mirrors lining the walls. This little box held all kinds of memories for him—none of them good.

"Karin?" he greeted his assistant when she picked up. "I want you to get onto Tony Ciaccetti and have him sort out the door security at Morningside."

It was crazy that the residents of his building had to pass messages up the stairwell like a warfront. It was secure enough, just not convenient. Which hadn't really troubled him before, but now that he saw it in action he realized how difficult it could make things, especially for older residents. Even for Tori.

Just because he'd dreaded the knell of the buzzer as child didn't mean every tenant in the place had to suffer the consequences.

He lurched to a halt on the eighth floor and optimistically pressed Tori's floor again. The doors opened then closed, and for one hopeful moment he thought the elevator was going to rise. But no, the doors reopened impotently, as silently judging as Tori was every time she'd mention some failing part of the building.

"I'll see you tomorrow, Karin."

He stepped out into the hallway and disconnected his call, then turned with determination to the stairwell before daring to lift his eyes again. Today he just didn't need the shadows of the apartment where he grew up. In the relative silence of the stairwell his ears tuned in to the steady thump of feet coming closer. He trod the two flights and held open the door with her floor number painted on it in flaking blue.

A moment later Tori appeared, sprinting heavily up the final flight. She jogged straight past him onto the tenth floor. She didn't smell nearly as bad as she probably feared. Actually she smelled pretty good. An image of rumpled sheets twisted his gut, rough and distracting, before he shut it down.

"I'm sure someone would have told me if we'd installed a gym in the building."

She slowed to a walk and let him catch up and spoke between heavy puffs of breath. "I run the stairs every day."

He looked at her, frowning. Significant heat stained her perfect skin, but it didn't detract from the fine lines of her bone-structure. "All twelve floors?"

"Three times each."

His feet ground to a halt. Well, that explained her legs. "Why not run the streets? The parks? You have enough of them nearby."

Her lashes dropped. "I don't like to run alone, even during the day." She pulled a key from a chain that hung disguised in cleavage he wouldn't have expected to be there and opened her front door.

Nate closed it behind them. "It's just dawned on me that you've been very relaxed about having me in your home. Given you don't know me from Adam. And given your…interest…in security."

If by *interest* one meant *fixation…*

"Relaxed? No." Her smile was tight. "But you own the building. I figure if you had anything nefarious in mind you could get a key to any of our doors without any difficulty." The smile mellowed into a sweet twist. "Or just kick it right in."

His gut twanged. Here was he imagining her naked and meanwhile she was finally softening to him.

Schmuck.

"I'm not sure, but that sounded almost like…trust?"

"Or resignation to my fate."

Her husky laughter heightened the streak of color still high in her cheeks. She stood straighter to pat a towel down the bare, glistening parts of her body. His own tightened. Just slightly. It had been a long time since any woman got anything other than designer-sweaty in front of him. Exertion just wasn't in with the women in his social circles. Except one kind of exertion and even that was often carefully orchestrated. Yet that wasn't what was holding his attention—at least not entirely.

It was the warmth in Tori's eyes. He hadn't realized before that anything had been missing from her steady gaze, but seeing it now full of light and laughter, he knew he'd miss it terribly if it vanished again.

"I'll take trust," he said.

They fell to silence, standing awkwardly in her neat living room, staring at each other.

"I should…" She waved her hands at her state of dress, then glanced around nervously.

She wanted to take a shower, but not while he was in her home. So trust was a measured thing, then. He crossed to the giant box dumped in the middle of her floor. If he couldn't get absent, he'd get busy. "I'll get your TV hooked up while you're gone."

"I hope that's all box," she said, eyeing the monolith. "I probably can't afford the electricity for anything bigger."

Again the vast gulf between them came crashing home to him. He hadn't even thought about running costs for a big-screen plasma. So maybe he wasn't still as attuned to his roots as he liked to believe. "It's mostly packing foam. Don't worry."

At least he really, really hoped so.

She shifted nervously, then seemed to make a decision, and disappeared into her bedroom. He heard the spray of water and then the very definite snick of a lock being turned. At least she hadn't consigned him to the hall as she had that first day.

He'd spent enough time in hallways for one lifetime.

He took the opportunity to look around. The floor plan was identical to the apartment he'd grown up in, two floors down, and beneath the layer of bright, contemporary paint he still recognized the essential design. Tori's careful application of color and light helped to make this stock-standard apartment into a cozy, feminine home. Much nicer than the one he grew up in.

On the mantel, she'd displayed a number of framed photographs: a blissfully happy-looking gray-haired couple in front of a large RV named Freedom; a stunning print of a bald eagle in flight silhouetted against a blazing sky and one of Tori herself, fully kitted up in climbing gear but relaxed and pouring two mugs of steaming coffee from a campfire pot and laughing up at the camera, her cheeks flushed with cold and vibrant life.

Her parents. Her mountains. And, presumably, her life. The look of total comfort and adoration on her face as she looked at whoever was taking the photo—whoever the second cup of coffee was for—squirreled down deep into his soul.

A lover?

Again the slither of jealousy coiled low in his belly. What kind of a man would Tori Morfitt choose? Not the beanie guy, surely. She'd appreciate someone outdoorsy, not too precious to pitch a tent out in the woods somewhere. Maybe an alpha type. A smart guy? A rich guy?

He looked around again, frowning. No other evidence that anyone else lived here with her or ever had. No photos of a man. More important…why was a creature as intrinsically *wild* as Tori Morfitt living in a cruddy building in upper Manhattan?

And…why did he care?

Behind him the shower shut off, so Nate got busy tearing into the shipping box his firm had delivered. He wrestled the

TV from its container, said a tiny whisper of thanks that it truly was moderate in size and busied himself disconnecting the old one.

By the time Tori emerged from her shower, clean and fresh and feeling infinitely more respectable in a T-shirt and jeans, Nathan was tuning the new television. It was spectacular. Not enormous, but flat-screen, which made it far less obtrusive in her small apartment than its clunky predecessor, which presently dominated the coffee table. That had been her parents' before they'd sold up everything and committed themselves to a life roaming around North America in their mobile home. She'd been happy to take it, though. She'd had to replace everything when she moved in here with only the bare essentials five years ago.

It had been years since she'd had anything shiny and new in her apartment. Just the smell of the packaging was exciting.

Pathetic, Morfitt.

Nathan spun around as she cleared her throat and spoke. "Wow. I may also have to introduce you to the tenants in the next building over for a truly fair trade."

Not that she knew anyone in the next building or could even visualize it anymore. She frowned.

He picked up the remote control and crossed to stand beside her. "Ready for a show?"

He thumbed the remote and the screen filled with the vision-feed from her ledge—just like the image in the bathroom monitor but vastly larger. Her ledge—complete with side-opening nest box, scattered substrate and scrubbed clean of pigeon poop—filled her living room in glorious high definition. On-screen, a curl of residual steam from her shower drifted out the open bathroom window.

"I should have done this years ago," Tori whispered as she sank into her sofa, misty-eyed. "It's awesome."

As they watched, a heavily feathered, brown-and-black hawk appeared on the edge of the screen. Nathan sucked in a breath.

Tori leaned sideways as though it might improve the framing, then she scooted to the front of her sofa.

"Wilma, I think."

He slid down next to her, just as captivated. "How can you tell?"

"Her coloring is different and she's smaller."

"That's small?"

Tori laughed. "She looks huge on screen, but peregrines are smaller than most of the other birds of prey. Fred's a good deal bigger than her. He needs to be to provide for his family."

Wilma's patterned head turned close to 360 degrees as she scanned her environment relentlessly, but her clawed feet took her closer to the box. Step by cautious step.

"She's here to check it out," Tori whispered.

They watched in silence—as though the slightest noise from inside the apartment would somehow disturb Wilma's investigations—and she patrolled the ledge, inching ever closer to the box. She plucked what little substrate was left out of the box and then stepped into it, exploring it thoroughly but keeping a hawk eye on possible predators.

Left of screen another dark blur touched down.

"Fred!" Tori leaned even farther forward and Nathan was right beside her. His thigh pressed hard against hers, drawing her glance down for a heartbeat. But she forced it up to watch the screen.

The larger bird had alighted on the ledge blurrily close to the camera. But they could still make him out as he crossed back and forth in front of the camera lens, studying this foreign arrival while Wilma continued to toss substrate out of the box in the background. The camera stayed focused on the nest box.

"Easy buddy…" Nathan whispered as Fred pecked at the lens with his savage hooked beak and gnawed on the rubber surround. But the bird's curiosity soon waned and he turned his attention to his mate. Wilma stood in the nest box apparently satisfied with what she had found.

Tori held her breath. In her peripheral vision she saw Nathan turn to watch her face. But she couldn't take her own eyes off the screen.

"Come on…come on…"

Then it happened. Casually as you like, Wilma picked up a random piece of tossed substrate from the ledge and carried it back to the box. She tossed it straight out again the moment she put it down, but then went and selected another more acceptable to her.

"What's she doing?" Nathan asked.

Tori's throat was too thick to speak. She swallowed hard and then tried again. "Starting a nest."

It was the most beautiful thing she'd seen. Up in the mountains she'd seen majestic aeries but they'd all been fully formed. Renovations of last year's eroded nests. This was the first time she'd seen a bird choose and build a nest from scratch.

And they'd chosen *her* ledge. If not for Nathan and his television she wouldn't have seen any of this.

She turned her face to him as Wilma continued searching for exactly the right piece of substrate. "This is so special. I'm so sorry I've been such a pain in the butt about all of this. Thank you, Nathan."

His blue eyes were steady, but somehow they made her critically aware of how naked she'd been just moments before as water sluiced down over her hot skin while he worked just beyond her bathroom wall. And how naked she would be now if not for the thin layers of cotton-blend fabric separating them. Yet his eyes never so much as left hers.

He smiled. "You know, I've been here three times and that's the first time you've said my name. I was beginning to wonder if you knew what it was."

Heat rushed up her newly showered neck. "Of course I knew it. It's on your business card…Nathan…" She stumbled to a halt, cursing that just using his name should feel so intimate. But it did. As though she'd whispered it. "I mean… Yes, I knew it. I'm sorry."

"I'm not after an apology. I just like the way you say it."

The pulse in her throat started to thump. In her periphery, the birds continued exploring the ledge. But a pterodactyl touching down to join them couldn't have torn Tori's gaze from his.

"How do other people say it?"

"Most people call me Nate. Or Mr. Archer."

This is where she should make a flippant comment about him being accustomed to being called *sir*. But flippancy was beyond her. She murmured instead, "What would you like me to call you?"

He stared at her for an eternity and her breath thinned out to almost nothing. He licked his dry lips and the tiny motion transfixed her. The last of her breath evaporated.

"Nathan is perfect," he finally said, husky and low. "Unique to you."

His phone trilled and the two falcons on-screen took urgent flight at the sudden sound through the bathroom window. She and Nathan snapped their focus to the empty screen and, when Tori's drifted carefully back, his had lost all hint of the warm depth she'd briefly glimpsed.

He silenced the trilling. "Archer."

His brows immediately dropped as he held the phone to his ear and then his lips tightened. He turned away from her but not before his eyes drifted shut with what looked like pain. Or exquisite relief.

"Thank you, Karin," he said quietly before hanging up. "I'll come right back. Yes, let him know I'll be right down."

"Bad news?" Tori said brightly, trying to drag things back on a professional footing. Trying to regulate her pounding heart.

"No. The opposite. A business deal I've been waiting on has finally come through."

"Oh. Well… Yay business!" She tightened her hands in her lap. Was she more annoyed that the phone call had interrupted the strange moment they'd almost shared or that he was so easily yanked away from it?

"Anyway," he said, sliding his phone back into his coat pocket and clearing his throat, "Nathan it is. It seems awkward if I'm calling you Tori and you're calling me Mr. Archer."

Tori's stomach dropped away. *Awkward.*

Huh.

Just like this moment.

What had just happened? What had just ended before it began? There was no hint now in Nathan's body language of the momentary connection she'd felt. Or had she imagined it? Could she be that sad?

"Will they be back?" He nodded his head at the television.

The birds. That's right…the whole point of them being here together.

"I'll liberate some straw from Marco deCosta's gerbil," she said, as eager to move on as Nathan suddenly seemed to be. Maybe his eyes had dropped closed with sheer relief that they'd been interrupted by the phone call? "Hopefully Wilma will like that more than the substrate."

He stood, almost stumbling in his haste. "I need to cut today's visit short, I'm sorry. I'll see you tomorrow."

Tori shook her head back to full sensibility, reluctantly stepping free of the fine threads of attraction that had unexpectedly tangled around her feet.

It took him about fifteen seconds to gather himself together and disappear out the door, and Tori got the feeling if there'd been a big red eject button in her apartment he seriously would have thought about pressing it to get out of here more quickly. She held the door open for him and he was through it and gone before she could do more than hastily say goodbye.

Wow. The last time she'd had that effect on a man, she was eighteen and Rick had warned off one of her friends so badly he'd practically paled when she next spoke to him. And given that her overprotective brother wasn't around to scare off any man who looked sideways at her, she could only assume she'd managed to put Nathan Archer off all by herself.

Which was fine, since she wasn't keen to indulge the schoolgirl flutters she got whenever he was around, but still…

That took a particular breed of talent.

* * *

His car pulled up in front of the building and Nate leaped in, hoping that Tori wasn't watching out her window. He really didn't need any more rich-guy black marks from her this week.

"Mr. Archer," his driver said.

"Hi Simon. Back to the office, please."

He felt an indescribable fraud turning up at his childhood building in the company limo. Like some guy who'd spent a month's wages hiring the car for the day to make a good impression. Except he had another one just like it in Sanmore's parking garage and no one to make a good impression on, particularly.

If anything, it would have made a bad impression on Tori had she seen it. He'd never thought he'd be more self-conscious of having money than he ever was of not having it. But then he'd never thought he'd be hanging out in his old building again, either.

The streets of Morningside and then the Upper West Side cruised by as the limo headed downtown. Nate pulled up the document Karin had emailed him and read it through twice. Confirmation that his demolition strategy had finally been approved by the city. A year's worth of negotiations and compliance hoop-jumping in order that he could redevelop his building in Morningside. The building he'd grown up in. The building Tori and all her batty neighbors now lived in.

But not for long.

He'd bought the building because he could. It had been a suitably poetic use for his first bunch of profit zeros. More than cars or women or planes—to buy out the building that they'd been so poor in and know that no-one could ever take it away from them. And becoming his mother's landlord…

Stupidly gratifying.

He'd never before—or again—felt so valued by Darlene Archer as he had the day she'd realized she could hit him up for free rental. It was as though he'd finally been some good to her. After she took her last selfish breath, he'd closed up her apartment and focused one hundred percent of his attention on to growing Sanmore Holdings. It wasn't until Dean had quizzed him about this sole piece of real estate in his portfolio three years ago that he'd started to wonder what else he could put on this site. Something shiny and modern. Something with a future…

…and no past.

The practical demolition application had been easy enough to get through City Hall but recent changes to the Tenancy Act meant he had to give the thirty-five households in his building more notice than he wanted to once the idea of development had taken root. And now that he held the actual permissions in his hands he wasn't prepared to wait at all.

He'd rehouse all thirty-five families in the Ritz if it meant getting this building emptied faster. They could live out the final months of their lease elsewhere courtesy of Sanmore Holdings and he could get on with upgrading the site. The bomb it would cost was more than worth it.

The fact his memories would finally be exorcised from his soul…pure bonus.

Simon pulled the limo up in front of Nate's Columbus Circle office tower to let him out before driving off to do the complicated four-block double-back to access the building's rear car park. With the downtown traffic and the monolithic Trump Towers next door, Nate would be at his desk before Simon even started heading back this way.

Karin met him at the elevator, her handbag on her shoulder and a guilty expression on her face.

"Nice to see you were sticking around in case I needed anything," Nate said dryly.

"It's Friday night, Nathan Archer. Just because you have no life doesn't mean all of us want to work late. I have babies to feed."

She rattled off a few of the afternoon's highlights and thrust a document into his hands. "How did it go?" Her kind eyes knew him so well. "Hostilities ceased?"

Viktoria Morfitt.

"We don't have to be best friends, Karin. I'll just do my time and we'll be back to our regular programming at Sanmore."

Karin lifted a single brow. "Uh-huh."

He'd worked with his assistant long enough to know most of her nuances. She saved her best Harlem gestures for when she had a real point to make. He leaned forward and pushed the down button on the elevator for her. "It's going to be fine."

"You don't have time for this, Nate. You have the merger and the StarOne software trials coming up this month."

"Don't frown at me Karin. I'm the Good Samaritan on this one." He jiggled the elevator button again.

"So fight it. You have right on your side."

He still could. Dean had the appeal paperwork sitting in a file just in case. But standing in Viktoria Morfitt's apartment this afternoon as his body answered the call of all her post-workout pheromones he knew he wouldn't be changing his mind.

There was just something about her. Something he needed some time to figure out.

But arguing with Karin in the hallway wasn't going to get him that. "Okay, I'll go talk to Dean."

"Thank you," Karin said with all the righteousness of a mother of four who was right very often. Except not this time. "Have a good night. Don't stay too late."

She said that every night. And every night he said, "I won't."

But the amount of work he left for her in the mornings probably told her a whole different story.

Nate saw her safely into the elevator and then turned down the hall away from his own office and poked his head around the door of his best friend's.

Dean looked up from whatever legal tome he was reading. "Hey. You're back early."

"Can you have your team get onto something for me?" The two of them had a lot of history together, but their friendship worked so well because they both knew how to maintain clean lines between work and personal.

Dean snapped straight into employee mode. "Name it."

Nate rattled off his plan for rehoming his Morningside tenants to expedite the demolition. Paying out their lease and finding alternative accommodations for every one of them.

"Expensive," Dean murmured. In the circles they both moved in vast dollars didn't scare them but they were still noted.

Nate countered. "Worth it, though."

He watched the lawyer in Dean war with the friend in him. They'd been through so much together. Everything.

"Yeah, it probably is," Dean said with a sigh. "I'll take care of it."

Nate's shoulders instantly lightened up. "Thanks, buddy. I'll give you more information as I can. Good night. Go home and start your weekend."

Back in his own office, Nate signed off on the few things Karin had left for him and returned one quick phone call to an overseas banker. Someone had said "The world never sleeps' and it was never truer. There were half a dozen ways the world could get hold of Sanmore's CEO, 24/7—office phone, home phone, cell phone, email, text, Twitter, couriers—and often at the same time. There hadn't been such a thing as *silence* on this planet since the internet was first wrestled from the hands of the military and went public.

But since he was as responsible for that as everyone else involved in the online boom he really couldn't complain.

He moved over to his floor-to-ceiling windows and stared out at Columbus Circle, but it didn't take long for his eyes to track right…uptown towards Morningside. Towards Tori.

She was someone who would appreciate silence.

Lots of silence.

He could imagine her scaling the face of some mountain with nothing but the sounds of her own exertion and the wind in her ears. No phones. No email. No relentless accessibility.

What would that be like?

He could have a taste of it if he turned off his phone when he was at her place. If he took the subway instead of the car so no one knew where he was. It would be as close to invisible as he got. As close to private. Although being *private* with Tori Morfitt was not necessarily a good idea.

As tempting as it was.

CHAPTER FOUR

"SETTLE, GRETEL."

The humongous dog returned to her mat in Tori's living room and curled back up in a neat, gigantic heap.

"Good girl."

Gretel's big brown Great Dane eyes watched every move Tori made and blinked happily from time to time before finally closing for yet another doggie nap. Life would be so much easier if humans could get away with napping as much as dogs did.

"It's a rough life, kid," Tori murmured, working at her computer on her latest falcon images.

Thirteen out of fourteen days Gretel's owners, the Radcliffes, managed to coordinate their respective work so one of them was home to feed, love and walk their small horse of a dog during the day. Every second Saturday that was Tori's job. Except for the walking part, but Gretel didn't seem to mind the absence of exercise just that once. She happily traded it for pats and snacks on Tori's mat. And Tori traded Gretel's nurse mother, Tracey, for medical assistance, as she needed it. So far, she hadn't really required more than checkups, flu advice and the occasional herbal for when her insomnia was particularly bad. And for anything bigger there were house-call medical services.

Thank God for New York. A supplier for everything, no need too obscure. On call 24/7. The relentless, too-close noise of the city was a small price to pay for that kind of service.

She fiddled with the saturation on a particularly pretty digital shot of Wilma landing on the ledge, some tufts of feather and twig in her hooked beak during her first, aborted, nest-building phase. Nathan wanted lots of images for the website, to make it really special. Fortunately, although she lacked the technical expertise to make this website a reality, gorgeous photos she could definitely provide. In abundance.

Gretel let out a corker of a snore over on her mat.

"Nice, Gretel," Tori twisted her lips but didn't take her attention off screen. "Your dad teach you those manners?"

By midafternoon, she filed away the last of the images she'd selected for the website and glanced at her watch. Her heart gave a little lurch. Nathan would be here soon and her tranquil afternoon would be shot. He'd swan in, dominate her apartment, her time and generally take up clean air. Then he'd find some unique way of making her feel inadequate and remind her of how busy and important he was, and his work would be done!

And all the while she'd be mooning about how good he smelled or looked in a suit.

Crazy.

Tori snapped her attention away from the blank wall and forced it back onto the computer. She had time, maybe she could do a bit of Mrs. Arnold's memories album. Yet another trade. This one for clothing alterations. Most of the catalogue clothes she ordered fitted just fine around her hips but were a bit loose around her waist. She still had a small, hard, climber's midriff courtesy of the ab cruncher hooked to the base of her bedroom door—fabulous for fashion but not if you wanted your pants to stay up. Mrs. Arnold was a deft touch with a sewing machine and—thanks to her desire to have her memories captured digitally, which she was *not* a deft hand with—kept all Tori's pants politely in position by way of thanks.

She glanced at her watch again. *Screw it.* This was her Saturday, too…she wasn't going to wait around for someone to call up the stairwell to tell her Nathan had arrived. He wasn't the only one whose time was worth something. She fired up her image software and the screen peppered with Mrs. Arnold's long lifetime of scanned memories. But then, down in the corner of the screen, another folder displayed by default—her personal one—and Tori fought hard to ignore it. But the more she ignored, the more it seemed to pulse and grow. Begging her attention. Without taking her eyes off Mrs. Arnold's black-and-white wedding photos, her hand slid the cursor over to her personal folder and readied to shush it back to where it came from.

But her fingers didn't make the minute depression needed to click the file shut. They hovered anxiously over it instead. She glanced around the room as though someone would catch her looking and then, with tight breath, slid her wrist slightly to the left and clicked. The whole time frowning, knowing this wasn't smart. Knowing it was going to hurt.

But unable not to.

Mrs. Arnold's folder minimized, and Tori's personal images unpacked like a picnic on her screen. Her life in rich, high-res pixels. Tori as a child, dirty and bloody and having a fabulous time down some hole or another. Her school friends, always trying to turn Tori into the girl she resisted being. Images of her gray-haired parents sent from all over America, each one crazier than the one before, most of them featuring some oversized monument on some long, busy interstate. The adventure of their lifetime. Love saturating each one.

Then Rick's folder. The one she tried to avoid but knew she wouldn't.

One click spilled her brother's beautiful face across her screen. Rick smiling. Rick on horseback. Rick looking back down to her from halfway up a rock face, the wind in his brown, tossed hair, the world in his bright, living eyes. So much like her own. The ache in her chest swelled out to encircle her lungs, too, stealing her breath. She'd taken all of these pictures. They'd spent so much time together and she'd captured so much of it by habit she literally had hundreds of photographs of her twin stored in her computer. But none in her apartment.

Losing him all over again in the waking moments of every day was hard enough without stretching it out across twelve hours. She liked to keep the memories contained.

She looked at them now, her mouse-finger clicking through all the different versions of her brother. Happy Rick. Frustrated Rick. Crazy Rick. Triumphant Rick. Rick in crisis. Rick in love. She'd grown up in his pocket and then shared a house with him until they were twenty-one—there wasn't an expression he had that she hadn't memorized.

Including the one in the split second when he'd realized he was going to die.

Behind her, something screeched and she jumped almost as high as Gretel who issued an urgent bark before galloping to the door. Heart thumping, she spun around and stared at her kitchen counter. Specifically at the great pile of cookbooks that were stacked there against the wall, against the—

The books buzzed again.

Tori quickly shifted the books and a vase of Mr. Chen's fresh-cut flowers away from the defunct intercom and stared at it as though it were alien technology. In so many ways it was. It had never worked in for five years here. Now it was making noise all of a sudden.

"Hello?" She pressed the blue button and shouted overly loud into the speaker. Alexander Bell couldn't have done better.

"Tori? It's Nate. Can you buzz me in?"

She blinked at the unit and muttered to herself. "I have no idea." She poked the blue button again and spoke loudly into the box. "Why is this working?"

His pause reeked with frustration. "I had it fixed." She heard him rattle the front door. "Try again."

She depressed the button marked with a bell and heard a clicking sound. He didn't call her back so she assumed he was in the building.

Her eyes went to the door where Gretel stood like a sentinel, eyeballs fixed on the shiny timber. It took her a few seconds to realise she was staring with the same vigilance, her heart pattering away in anticipation of Nate's brisk, confident knock.

"Do you have no pride?" she said to a tail wagging Gretel, but really it was for herself. She forced her attention back to her kitchen counter, now in disarray. Now that it was fully exposed, the intercom was really quite dusty so Tori quickly wiped it down and then set about making alternative space for her cookbook collection. She moved the flowers down to the coffee table.

First CCTV and now a working intercom. Way too much technological excitement for one week.

Gretel issued one of her booming barks and Tori snapped her head around to her apartment entrance as her heart burst into a furious thumping. She shoved her hip between the excited dog and the door and used her weight to force Gretel out of the way so she could open the door inwards, muttering to her, "It's not your parents, dopey. Too early."

Gretel's booming bark must have prewarned him, but still Nathan's eyebrows almost disappeared into the hair flopping over his forehead when he stepped into her apartment and saw the size of her other guest. He warily eyed the grinning, drooling monster that followed him in.

"I hope you get something amazing in return for that," he said, and then looked up at her. "What?"

Tori stared. He had exchanged his dark, tailored corporate clothes for a faded New York casual—well-loved jeans bunched around beaten boots, an earthy green hooded sweat, and a short suede jacket that matched the boots. His hair was finger-combed and loose, and free of whatever fifty-dollar-a-tube product usually kept it architecturally perfect. No doubt a lot of money went into making him look as though he'd just been throwing a ball for kids in the park. But it sure was well-spent.

For the first time, the gulf between them seemed to shrink. Monday-to-Friday Nathan screamed *hands off* in a way that made sidelining her hormones possible. But Saturday Nathan…

Her eyes tracked him into her tiny apartment. Breathless awareness surfed down her arteries, spreading a chaos of confusion to every cell in her body. She straightened self-consciously, just shy of giving Gretel a run for her money in the drool stakes.

…*this* Nathan was positively edible.

He courteously offered the dog the back of his hand, and Gretel swung around to give it an investigatory sniff, her muscled tail waving frantically. Tori snapped clear of her hormonal haze and dived for the coffee table just as the Dane's tail whipped the footing out from under the flowers she'd just moved there. In spite of her keen reflexes, the vase and its contents went flying. Water surged over the edge of the table and trickled onto the floor, but before she could do more than shout Gretel's name in exasperation, Nate tossed his jacket aside, hauled his sweater off and pressed it straight down into the spreading puddle, stemming the flow onto her carpet.

By the time Tori had wrestled an excited Gretel back to her mat and got her to drop and stay, Nate had the spill well and truly under control and three of the loose cut flowers in his hand. She joined him and picked up a few more from the floor. His sweatshirt was a ruined, soggy mess on the table, leaving him in just his T-shirt. Tori struggled not to appreciate the way the cotton fitted to his well-shaped torso and concentrated on plucking errant flower stalks from her sofa.

She'd hung out with climbers; buff torsos weren't anything new to her. Maybe it had just been a long time since she'd seen one. That's why her pulse was falling over itself suddenly.

That and the fact that he smelled different today. Killer cologne. She filled her lungs with his scent. Something…woodsy. She stared at him curiously. *Woodsy?* Why the change from his slick Fifth Avenue original?

"A dog like that should be out in the suburbs," Nathan said, breaking the silence she only just realized had stretched out.

"It was my fault. I shouldn't have put the flowers so low."

He straightened and stared at her. "Wow. I broke your door and you took me to court. Godzilla over there destroys your furniture and you give it full amnesty."

Heat threatened to peek over her collar. "*Gretel* didn't mean to do it."

"Excitement of the moment?"

Tori frowned, knowing exactly the same could be said for the day he broke her door down. "Okay, look. I'm sorry about everything that happened. You came lurching at me when I was out on the ledge. It freaked me out and I…" *I really don't like surprises.* "I may have overreacted a bit."

"Just a bit?"

"You have no idea how smug you were standing in that hallway with two cops eating out of your hand."

He glanced up at her. "Smug? Not something I was aware was in my professional repertoire."

"Seriously? No one's told you that before? You have this whole…lip-twist thing going on. It's extremely irritating."

Just like the tiny smile he gave her now. The way he saw right through her. His eyes sparkled. "Getting under your skin, Tori?"

Yes.

The toss of her head said the idea was laughable. "No. But you seem to be very accustomed to getting your own way. I don't like that in a person." God, she'd so nearly said *man*. Was his lumberjack cologne messing with her mind now, as well?

He studied her hard and finally spoke. "If I've railroaded you with anything, I apologize. Occupational hazard."

Should she tell him about that other annoying look he had—the whole innocent and earnest thing? Trouble was *that* look actually worked on her. Like right now. She thrust out her hand. "Give me your sweater, I'll wring it out."

"I'm here for a few hours. Hopefully it will dry out in that time."

In her north-facing windows? Not a chance. She wrung the

worst of the water out in her kitchen sink. "I'll take it up on to the roof—it'll get more sun there. Gretel needs a toilet stop anyway."

"You toilet the dog on the roof?" His cautious glance spoke volumes. "Is that hygienic?"

She had to laugh. "It's fine, Nathan. Wait and see."

It *was* fine. The roof was a mini haven for the residents of their building. One of the first things Tori had done when she moved in was install a big patch of turf alongside Mr. Chen's rooftop vegetable garden. Just turf—but a lush, large, elevated square. Mr. Chen let her piggyback off his reticulation and the Davidson kids' two pet rabbits kept the patch mowed with their daily visits and fertilized with their castings, so, while Gretel's fortnightly visits weren't great for it, it had plenty of recovery time in between.

"This is amazing," Nate said, looking around the crowded roof space. Tori's turf, Mr. Chen's veggies, a couple of deck-chairs, a small outdoor table, an empty wading pool, a washing line, and a rickety old telescope. It was a hive of activity—when it wasn't just the two of them.

Gretel crossed immediately to the grass, sniffed around briefly and did what she'd come for. While Nathan looked around, Tori carefully pegged his sweater on the sunny side of the washing-line to swing in the breeze.

"It wasn't like this when I liv—" He frowned darkly and flicked his eyes back to her. "When I bought the building."

Tori kicked off her shoes. "I wanted something to tend. I'd helped Mr. Chen build his vegetable garden so he helped me make this." She stepped onto the grass across from where Gretel had peed and sunk her bare toes into the thick green blades. Amazingly healthy given its containment. Although not given the massive amount of spoiling it got from Tori. It had to be the most expensive patch of lawn on Manhattan, inch-for-inch.

"I guess Gretel benefits," he smiled. "Of course, you know there's a park right at the end of the street?"

Her belly balled up tight and she frowned. "Right. But

Gretel's not mine and we weigh almost the same, I'd hate to lose her out in the street if something happened."

Nate's gaze narrowed but he accepted her word. "She seemed easy enough to handle on the stairs."

"That's because she was coming up. You wait till we have to take her back down."

Nate followed Tori's gaze to the dog and then upward to the telescope. He crossed to it and swung it around to look back toward lower Manhattan. "I'd forgotten what the view was like up here," he murmured.

"Not a patch on your office's outlook, I'm guessing."

He lifted his eyes and rested them on her. "Depends on what you value looking at."

For the life of her she couldn't tear her own eyes away. The air suddenly thinned like that on the highest mountain peaks and screws she barely knew she had began to tighten deep and low inside her. But then Gretel trotted over and saved the day, nudging Tori for a pat, providing the perfect, polite excuse to break the traction of Nathan's gaze.

"I prefer the rivers and parks," she said, slightly breathless. The upstate wilderness she hadn't visited since she'd lost Rick.

He swung the telescope around toward Riverside and picked out a few highlights to study. The rising arc of the telescope told her he'd spotted a hawk just before he asked "Why didn't you build your nest box up here?"

A tiny part of her mourned the return to the subject of the falcons. It only reminded her of the real reason he was standing with her on this roof. Duress. Couldn't they go on pretending they were just…friends…a little bit longer?

"Too exposed. They like cover on a couple of sides if they can. Also too much traffic up here."

He straightened. "Well, let's ease the congestion, shall we? Your website isn't going to design itself."

Tori sighed and followed him to the stairwell door, whistling for Gretel to follow. It took both of them to manhandle the dog back inside once she realized her rooftop visit was being cut unnaturally short, but she finally acquiesced.

On the tenth floor, Tori tossed her key to Nate.

"It's about time for me to drop her home," she said, her hand on the dogs smooth, warm head. "Let yourself in, I'll be right back."

Nate watched as she wrestled the small pony down the next flight of stairs. She hadn't been kidding when she'd spoken of the difficulty she'd have out in public if Gretel took it into her head to bolt. It was possible the dog actually *did* weigh more than its lithe human companion. She might have the taut array of climber's muscles, but Tori Morfitt was still half air.

And she blew as hot and cold as the most changeable winds. Today—lukewarm; he felt vaguely welcome. Maybe she mellowed on weekends? Maybe the presence of the dog chilled her out a bit? Whatever, standing on the roof with her was the first time he'd felt any kind of mutual respect between them. A reciprocal connection. Not the connection he kept stumbling over—the one he had no business feeling—but an intellectual one. Today he felt truly relaxed in her company.

He frowned and stumbled to a halt. *In this building.*

The residents had done something special up on that rooftop. Not complicated, not high-tech, but special. And clearly most of his tenants loved to spend some time up there. Just one more thing that would press on his conscience the day the demolition crew moved in.

Still, they were all on leases. Every single one of them knew nothing was forever.

Tori's door swung noiselessly inwards and Nate propped it open with a footstool, then poured himself a coffee from the simmering pot in the kitchen and made himself comfortable at Tori's computer ready for a long haul of web design. He was sure she had assumed he'd build the website in the comfort of his own home, on his own laptop, and then just upload it, finished, to her PC. That had been his plan, too, right up until the moment he found himself giving the doorman of his building a farewell salute this afternoon and turning left for the subway uptown. To Morningside. But, no. He was going to build the whole thing on her computer, downloading what he needed online, coding from scratch. The website he wanted to give Tori was old-school. Classic. Like her.

The long-forgotten rush of staring at a blank page of code hit him again now. Man, how long had he been out of his zone? Another thing he'd exchanged for success. He used to live on air and the thrill of programming back when he was starting out.

Nate wiggled the mouse to bring Tori's hibernating screen back to life and then sucked in a breath as he slowly sank back in his seat. Dozens of photos of the same man splayed out on the screen like a pack of cards. As if she'd just been poring over them in privacy. A good-looking, athletic man. A really happy man. A man literally on top of the world in some of the photographs.

A climber.

He flicked through them. Insanely, it had never seriously occurred to him that Tori might have a boyfriend. The absence of pictures in the apartment—of a man in the apartment—had given him a false sense of security. *Here* were the photos most girlfriends splashed all over their living rooms. Their phones. Their social networking accounts. The way the women he risked relationships with liked to carry him around like a social handbag.

A boyfriend. He'd been stupid to assume—

"What are you doing?

Her quiet, pained words brought him round sharply, as guilty as if he'd been caught digging through her underwear drawer. Heart thumping from way more than just the surprise of being caught.

Tori had a boyfriend.

"Sorry, were you working on something?"

The darkness of her gaze lifted slightly as she cleared her throat. "No. I was just…" She stepped forward and pressed slightly against him as she leaned in to close the file. The hairs right along that side of his body gravitated towards her. Her trembling hand missed the first attempt. But then the images sucked back into the file and disappeared into darkness. Which is exactly where she'd be hoping the subject could stay. He saw it in the way her eyes rested everywhere but on his.

He spun in the chair as she hurried into the kitchen to wash her hands. "Who was that, Tori?"

Her body stiffened and stumbled, but she forced her hands to reach for the simmering coffeepot.

He tried again. "Someone special?"

It had to be, the way she was going all out to pretend the images were of no consequence. She finished pouring her coffee and wiped down the spotless kitchen counter, then the coffeepot. Then a nonexistent mark on her refrigerator door. He watched her rinse the cloth thoroughly and lay it carefully over the edge of the sink to dry. He'd seen this kind of delay tactic in the boardroom; the corporate equivalent anyway. Silence was his best friend right now, he knew if he waited long enough she'd spill.

Eventually.

She turned to him, seemingly desperate for a task, and opened her mouth to ask him something, but her gaze fell on his still-steaming cup of coffee and the words dried up. But she was looking at him with speech trembling on her lips and he was steadily watching her. Waiting. She had to say something if she couldn't offer him a coffee.

She turned, reached into her tiny pastry, retrieved a packet of shortbread biscuits and placed a couple on a plate. Then, on still-bare feet, she brought him the offering and placed it silently next to him on her desk.

Still he waited.

The computer whirred, oblivious, in the awkward silence.

"My brother, Rick," she finally said.

Relief pumped through him in a steady, controlled feed. His eyes fell briefly shut. Not a boyfriend. Not a lover.

A brother.

Maybe all sisters kept hundreds of photos of their brothers. He wouldn't know, happy families were so far outside his field of experience.

He scrabbled around for something normal to fill the next silence. "Good-looking guy."

Pain flashed across her face in a hundred tiny muscle shifts and he knew, somehow, he'd said the wrong thing. Again.

"Yes."

"Good genes in your family."

The lameness of his words was only amplified by the silence with which they were met. *Christ, Archer, why don't you just ask her how she likes her eggs in the morning and be done with it...* He really was out of practice. How hard could it be to get someone to start talking about something more personal than the neighbors?

Attempt number two. "Where does he live?"

Tori stared at him, carefully neutral, then at the now-blank computer screen. Then she straightened and offered him a watered-down facsimile of a smile that barely twitched a cheek before speaking softly. "In my heart."

Nate's stomach sank. That explained the photos. "He's dead?"

She nodded.

When? How? And most importantly...*Are you okay?* But he only risked, "I'm sorry."

She lifted her coffee to her lips and her still-trembling fingers sloshed it in its cup. "Me, too."

"Were you close?"

She nodded again. Barely.

Okay, he was prepared to do this twenty-question fashion if he had to. The chance to peek inside Tori Morfitt's heart was too golden an opportunity to politely step back from. He scrabbled around for something lateral to ask.

"Did he teach you to climb?" Those photos that looked out over massive expanses of American landscape...

Tori's nostrils flared and she seemed to collapse in on herself like a tumbling building, walls of defense blocking him out. *Clang, clang, clang...*like the best system firewall, as the opportunities for him to advance slammed shut one by one. But he knew the best way through a crashing system was forward. Steady and unpanicked. Fewer mistakes that way.

"I taught him," she croaked.

Steady and unpanicked… "Did you both live in New York?"

"No. We're from Oregon." She was like a rusted piece of machinery oiled for the first time in thirty years. Slowly, painfully, her speech was coming more freely.

"Not from Manhattan?" he asked. Though he already knew the answer.

Her lips twisted and he almost heard the protesting squeak. "Most of Manhattan's not from Manhattan."

"I am." The words were out before he even knew they were forming.

Her almond eyes elongated and creased slightly at the corners. "I know. Your accent's a dead giveaway. Where did you grow up?"

His senses went on full alert. *Uh-uh. This is my inquisition, not yours.* "Not far from here. What part of Oregon?"

She leaned down over him and opened another photo album on the desktop. A heap of rugged wilderness shots scattered across the screen. Oregon, presumably.

"Medford, originally. Though Rick and I shared my grandmother's place on the edge of Portland when we moved out of home." Her conversation unwound along with some of the visible tension in her body.

"Good climbing district." He had no idea if that were true but she accepted it easily enough. "What brought you to New York?"

She stared long and hard. No longer tense but a million miles from relaxed. It only tweaked his instincts further. He wanted to tease the pain he could see right out of her, carefully and controlled. He wanted to see what she looked like without the perpetual shadow in her gaze.

"It wasn't Oregon."

He kept his smile light. "Florida would have been further."

"Geographically maybe."

Interesting. So what was she after by coming here? "Fresh start?"

"Something like that."

"Do you miss the wilderness?"

A sharp kind of pain flashed across her eyes, and then it was gone. "Every day."

"Why not go back?"

"There's nothing there for me now. After Rick… When he was gone, my parents sold up and hit the road. They're official Gray Nomads now."

"Was that their way of coping?"

A frown formed on her smooth brow. "It's their way of honoring Rick. By living their lives to the fullest."

"What's your way?"

The shutters dropped again. This time instant and entire. He'd pushed too far. But short of quizzing her on the finer details of how a healthy young man dies so young, he was going to have to ease back on trying to twist his way into her inner psyche. She'd tell him when she was ready.

Or not… Which would be quite telling in itself.

"They visited once but didn't like bringing the RV into Manhattan. We talk by phone all the time."

A spectacularly obvious change of subject but he let it go. "It's nice that you're close to your parents."

"Where's your family?"

Unprepared for the question, it took his defenses by surprise. A tiny thread of old pain took its chance and weaseled out between the cracks from the place he kept it carefully contained, tightening his whole body. "I'm all that's left."

Surprise lightened Tori's features, followed almost immediately by compassion. It was such a welcome change from the shadows he'd caused her he forgot to be defensive about her pity. "Really? I had imagined you as one in a big family of successful Manhattan achievers."

His snort rivaled that of the half-dog-half-horse that had just left. "No. I was born in the city but my mother wasn't. She moved here back in the eighties to pursue..."

Wow. How was he going to put this...?

"Her dreams?" Tori stepped in.

He couldn't credit the woman he remembered with possibly having aspirations and dreams. Certainly she'd never encouraged him to have any. "Her *job*. She never spoke of her family. Or where she'd come from." Or where he had. Though he had a pretty good idea about that.

"They're *your* family, too. You never asked about them?"

"All the time at the beginning. But my mother wasn't a woman who believed in looking backwards." Plus she had no idea at all which of dozens of men had actually fathered her child.

Tori stared. "Huh. Not what I imagined at all," she said.

Uncomfortable, suddenly, with the false image she must have had of his halcyon childhood in an up-market neighborhood surrounded by opportunity and wealth and love, he shifted decisively in the chair. He flicked casually through more of her on-screen photographs, scrabbling for a subject change.

"Is that Potsdam?" he asked, enlarging one of her images on-screen. It was a wilderness shot with a river twisting through the background and a pretty village on its banks taken from high up in a mountain range. "I went to school there. Clarkson. Upstate, at the base of the Adirondack Mountains. That's definitely New York State."

She leaned in over him slightly to look at the image, and her heat radiated deliciously. And her scent—lightly floral, intensely seductive.

"That's where I took it. I climbed the Adirondacks with—" She stumbled. "It looks like a beautiful place to go to school."

Six hundred acres on the banks of the Raquette River. "It was."

"Far from home." Her gray eyes slid sideways to search his. "Almost across the Canadian border."

"Almost across the universe. That's what I loved about it."

"You really weren't happy here. Why Clarkson?"

"Because they took me. I was early admission and on scholarship." *Hardship* scholarship seemed too pathetic to add.

"Early admission…? You must have been a bright kid."

"I studied and read relentlessly." And half the high-school faculty wanted him the heck out of his mother's orbit and, collectively, pulled every string they could to find him an opportunity.

"Then what happened?"

"I discovered the opposite sex." Those years at Clarkson were the first good years he'd ever had.

"And that was the end of the reading and the studying, I'm sure."

"Not at all. Every girl on campus wanted to take the young kid under their wing. They all thought I needed some kind of bridging tutoring. It was a great way to meet girls." A lot of girls. And volume meant he could keep them all at a nice, safe distance. Where they all belonged.

Tori laughed. "How early was your admission?"

"Only a year. But a year means a lot when you're seventeen. And I was happy not to let on that I was already aceing my classes."

Tori smiled. "My landlord, the player."

"Landlord?" He winced. "You make it sound like I have a paunch and a cardigan." It was more than just vanity that made him want that image of him stripped from her mind, permanently. He took a lot of pride in being a leader in the world's fastest-growing industry.

She backpedalled immediately. "Not at all. You're in great shape—"

The blush that stole up her neck only endeared her to him

more. Nate's lips twisted in exactly the way she hated. "Coming from a rock-climber that's quite a compliment."

"Ex rock-climber."

"You wouldn't know it. There's not an inch of fat on you."

Her eyes flew to his and flared as he watched. Okay, not his most subtle moment but totally worth it to see the dawning of awareness in her gray depths. Time slowed to molasses as he brushed his glance over every part of her face. The doe lashes. The smooth bridge of her nose with its peppering of freckles. The perfect shape of her mouth. Made for kissing…

As his focus lingered there, she sucked a corner of her bottom lip between pearly teeth, and tiny creases roosted in the corners of her eyes. Tiny, *anxious* creases.

He pushed away from the computer slightly, giving them both some much-needed oxygen. "How about you show me what you've pulled together for the website graphics and we'll start planning what kind of feel you want it to have? How we can bring the world into Morningside."

She regarded him thoughtfully, but then she crossed to the tiny dining alcove and selected one of two barely used chairs and brought it over to sit next to him. Close enough that her clothed arm pressed against his bare one, and her warmth radiated out and gently heated that part of him that was cold and empty from everything he'd not revealed.

A place where warmth seldom reached. Seldom survived.

He let the welcome glow soak in and did nothing to shift politely away. As she opened the computer file with her astounding falcon imagery he tried not to indulge the satisfaction of knowing that she hadn't moved away either.

She didn't like him smug.

CHAPTER FIVE

In late afternoon, the stairwell spat Nate out on the eighth floor and, as he always did, he kept his eyes low and headed directly for the elevator, intentionally avoiding the far end of the hall. But as he drew close to the silver antique he slowed… wavered.

He should check. What if the place had been vandalized? What if a water pipe had burst? What if someone had been secretly living here the entire time it had been boarded up? Going back into his mother's apartment was not high on his list of favorite things to do, but it was probably necessary. Besides, how long could he hang out in this building and pretend apartment 8B didn't exist?

He wiped his damp palms on his jeans as he walked down the hall, fished the cluster of keys out of his pocket and then slid the tarnished bronze one carefully into the lock.

And then he stopped.

Hand poised. Lungs aching. Just staring at the tarnished letter B that hung crookedly on the outside of the door.

Every miserable memory of the woman—the men, the drinking, the wailing and moaning, the *other* moaning, the fighting—it all came back to him in a blinding, sickly rush. He recalled every reason he'd ever sealed up this door and not looked back.

He braced his hands on the door frame and let his head sag forward. If the pipes were damaged or the place was full of vermin or squatters then that was going to have to be someone else's job to discover. He'd taken many risks in his life, overcome many hurdles; he didn't consider himself lacking in strength or courage, but nothing short of a force of nature was getting him through that door.

He pulled his phone out to get Karin to arrange an inspection.

"I think she's out," a quiet voice said behind him.

He turned to see a small, folded-over woman in a neat, faded dress.

A violent rattle started up deep inside. "I'm just…uh…"

"She's probably gone for cigarettes. Smokes like a chimney, that one." The old woman had a pruned smile, and bright, vacant eyes. Kind and deep but…vacant. And disturbingly familiar. Nate's stomach coiled tighter.

"Nancy! There you are." Tori's head popped out of the stairwell and huffed with relief. "I just got a call to say you were out. We've been looking for you all over the building."

The woman turned slowly. "I'm helping this delivery man. He needs someone to sign for the parcel for 8B."

Tori looked at Nate curiously, then glanced around for a delivery. There was no point denying it—that wouldn't help the older woman's confusion. Nancy's ancient gaze drifted to the phone he still held clutched in his hand. Clearly, she wasn't moving until he had a signature.

"I'll take care of that," Tori said, putting her hand out for the phone. She took it from him and pretended to sign it. The old woman smiled again and stepped closer. Nate froze as the complicated mix of smells reached out to him. Talcum powder. Citrus. And old lady.

"Would you like to come on up with me?" she said to him.

His chest clenched. Immediately. Painfully.

Conclusively.

"We'd love to, Nancy, thank you," Tori soothed. "It's a long climb. Will you be okay?"

"The elevator's broken," she said, curling her arm for Tori to take.

His gut squeezed again. Something clearly was not right here.

"I know," Tori said. "But we'll help you. Wait a moment, Nancy, while I get the door." She moved down the hall. Nate took the older woman's arm.

"Miss Smith?" He hadn't meant to say it out loud and he barely did. The ancient ears certainly didn't hear him and neither did Tori. She was too busy propping the stairwell door open twenty feet away.

Would you like to come up?

It had become a regular offer when she'd step out of the lift on the eighth floor to swap to the stairwell and find Nate there, curled against the wall after school while his mother… worked. Nancy, according to Tori, but he'd only ever known her as Miss Smith. He spent the better part of most afternoons hanging out at her place—doing his homework, watching TV, watching her cook a meal. Occasionally he'd slept on her sofa when his mother went out all night and forgot to leave the key for him. Although he'd never eat with her no matter how hungry he was or how amazingly good her food smelled. Accepting sanctuary was one thing; accepting charity…

God, he hadn't thought about her in years. He hadn't let himself.

They were one long, exhausting flight up before she lifted her thin silver curls to look at Nate. "I should sign for that parcel."

"Perhaps when we get to your door," he said, lending her as much of his strength as he could and glancing over her head at Tori, who smiled tightly at him.

It took close to ten minutes to shuffle her up to the twelfth floor. Nate had long since realized that this was the eighty-something-year-old woman Tori had referred to on the first day they'd met. She was right. This climb would kill Miss Smith one day.

He held her arm tighter.

"Here we are," Tori smiled as they emerged on to the top floor of the twelve-story building. Nate's chest cramped up hard. God knows how the old lady's must be feeling. But his chest-squeeze was uncomfortable for way more than just his exertion, as twenty years in full tackle gear rushed headlong at him.

"You left your door open," Tori gently admonished as they stepped Nancy across the hall to 12C's entry.

He looked around. Nothing about this place had changed one bit. The furniture was even still where it had been two decades before. Like a museum display built to haunt him. But Miss Smith was changed. Had she always been this tiny? She made Tori seem positively robust. Or had he just grown so much?

In a building where everything felt as recent as last week, seeing Miss Smith so aged was a shock. A reminder that time actually had passed since that day when he was seventeen and he'd walked out of this building without a backward glance. He'd never even said goodbye to Miss Smith.

"Lemonade, dear?"

His head came up fast enough to give him whiplash, but she wasn't speaking to him. She was smiling at Tori, who closed the door carefully, properly, behind them.

That was straight out of his childhood, too. Miss Smith's lemonade. A sweet, tangy port in the relentless storm of his miserable childhood.

"I'd love some, Miss—" The words *Miss Smith* so nearly spilled from his lips until he remembered that he only knew her first name as far as Tori was concerned. "Nancy. Thank you."

Tori caught his eye apologetically as the older woman wandered into her kitchen. He split his frozen lips into something he hoped resembled a smile. But Tori's frown suggested maybe he hadn't quite pulled it off.

She dropped her voice. "I'm sorry Nathan. I hope this won't take long."

"She's got Alzheimer's?"

She glanced toward the kitchen. "Dementia. Mild enough she can still live on her own, but severe enough she might wander out of the building and forget where she lives. She's been stable for a few years, but it's been worse this past year. Inside her apartment she's generally okay. Or in the building. Everyone here looks out for her." Her eyes narrowed slightly. "You're extremely special. She would normally never invite a stranger up. Ever."

Nathan averted his eyes immediately and, grief welling, watched the tiny, blue-rinsed woman pottering in her kitchen. Miss Smith had given him shelter when he'd needed it—never a question asked—and he'd barely thought of her these past two decades. He remembered her as old twenty years ago, but logically she could only have been in her mid-sixties back then. Somewhere deep in his subconscious he'd convinced himself she'd have died by now. So to find her still living, but in such poor health… And all alone…

"Here you are, dear. No sugar." She reappeared and passed one of two tall glasses of home-squeezed lemonade to Tori, and then turned to him. "And extra for you."

Nate reeled as the soft, wrinkled hands extended a pebbled glass straight from his past. Extra sugar. Just how he'd always taken it. He glanced up between chest thumps but her pale eyes showed no recognition whatsoever. Whatever functioning part of her clouded brain remembered how he took his lemonade, it wasn't communicating with the part that would remember a face. Or a name. Or, God forbid, his circumstances.

She remembered him, but apparently she didn't.

His hand shook as he took the glass, and his eyes flicked to Tori.

She glanced openly and quizzically between him and Miss Smith. He didn't dare hold the older woman's gaze in case the spark of recognition should suddenly form. In case she'd remember and blurt out what she knew. Instead, he took his lemonade and wandered over to the window to look out, keeping his back firmly to her.

The view didn't do much of a job of taking his mind off the imminent exposure that he risked by staying, but storming out now would only make it all more dramatic and obvious. The last thing he wanted or needed was for Tori to start asking questions about his childhood. He was as changed from the boy he'd been as Miss Smith was from the woman he remembered, but even through the haze of dementia she had recognized him on some unconscious level.

Tori sipped her lemonade and made quiet conversation with his old friend. Her tranquil goodness radiated outward and made him feel positively grimy for the kind of life he'd led here, for the decisions he'd made since leaving.

There was a reason he didn't like to go back into those feelings. They weren't productive.

The ice in his glass rattled and he realized how brutally he was holding his lemonade. He took a long, careful swig and half drained the contents, wincing. Memories flowed into him with the bittersweet liquid. The taste of citrus on his tongue as a boy, had become a balm against what he knew was going on downstairs, a psychological bridge to safety that he could cross as the drink crossed his lips, to enter Miss Smith's pillowed world. Somewhere normal. A thousand miles from the apartment four floors down where his mother sold her body to strangers three times a day.

Mission accomplished. These days he had money bursting out of metaphorical suitcases. More than any of them ever could have imagined. The life he lived now couldn't have been more different to the first two decades of his existence.

"Are you finished?" Tori's soft voice brought him around. She took his half-empty glass from his cold fingers. The warmth he'd admired earlier had completely vanished and a flat caution filled her expression instead. Understandable, given he'd been treating her to his back for the past ten minutes.

He nodded. "Let's get out of here." It was straight from his aching heart. From the part of him that still carried shame. But it visibly pierced her skin.

Her brows dropped and her eyes darkened. "I'm sorry to have kept you. But thank you for helping me get her back upstairs."

Disapproval leached through the tightness of her expression. She couldn't understand his haste, of course. She had no idea how many agonies it was for him, standing here, smelling these smells, reliving the memories. So unprepared.

In front of *her.*

"I'll start on the website tomorrow afternoon," he murmured. There was no way he could stay today.

"It's Sunday."

"Doesn't matter. The faster I get this done…" *The faster I get the hell out of this building.*

A dark shaft flashed across her face. "Right. Of course. Time is money."

He nodded his farewell, glanced at Miss Smith and hurried out into the relative silence of the hallway where his memories didn't shriek at him.

As he pushed open the stairwell door, he imagined Miss Smith's frail wrists trying to do it. Remembered how they'd had to proceeded slowly as a funeral cortège up the four flights from the eighth floor where she'd found him. He kept his eyes down as he switched from the stairs to the elevator, but then made himself raise them as he stepped in. He couldn't go on studying the carpet forever.

He glanced around at the aged inner furnishings and let himself go back where he seldom did. His sixteenth birthday. The cheaply dressed woman turning to him with a smile as fake as the nails that stalled the elevator in middescent. How he'd pressed his clenched fists to the polished glass throughout the whole encounter—wanting it and hating it at the same time—and stared into the reflection of his own anguished, fevered eyes until it was over.

But he never forgot it, nor forgave the woman who'd caused

it—not the stranger who'd popped the gum back into her mouth and tottered on high heels out of the elevator ahead of him, but her…his mother…the woman who'd gifted fifteen minutes of a fellow hooker's time to Nate for his sixteenth birthday. One of the rare times she'd given him anything.

And it had broken the final surviving fragment of his embittered young heart.

The next time he saw Darlene Archer was at her funeral. Dean's parents had offered him a no-questions-asked spare bed until his college scholarship kicked in. For months he'd been a model houseguest for them, so much so that Dean's mother had had to beg Nate not to do so much around the house. But he'd ignored her pleas; he was so desperate to stay. So damned desperate not to go back.

The lurch of the elevator snapped his thoughts back to the present. He shouldered his way through the aging doors and into the foyer before they were fully open, longing for fresh air all of a sudden. This was exactly why he'd locked those memories deep inside. It was bad enough growing up with the crippling lack of affection and interest from his mother. He didn't want to drag the anchors with him into his adult years.

And he hadn't. He'd stayed focused and on track right through college and into his career. That focus had brought him everything he wanted.

His mind threw up an image of the judgment leaching from perceptive gray eyes in Nancy Smith's apartment.

He pulled out his phone and dialed his office with unsteady fingers. "Karin," he said, and then cleared his voice so she could hear him more clearly. "Get someone to repair the elevator at Morningside, will you?"

Karin chose her words carefully. "That's not going to be cheap, Nathan. And you've just pressed the green light on demolition. Are you sure?"

It was unlike her to second-guess him, but then again, it was unlike him not to sound certain, to be reacting on emotion and not sound business sense. But his interest in making

Nancy Smith's day that little bit easier belonged one hundred percent in the past. His conscience and his judgment warred in a funnel of turbulent emotion deep inside. This was exactly why he never let emotion interfere with business.

He swore. "Get me three quotes, then. I'll see whether it's worth it." Then, because his assistant had been with him through thick and thin and because none of this was her fault, he softened his voice. "Thanks, Karin."

But somewhere deep inside he knew he'd do it. Or something better than fixing the elevator. He could make a difference for the woman who'd made such a difference to him, albeit years too late. He'd make sure she was re-housed somewhere better than his crappy old building—so she could be comfortable for the last years of her life.

It wasn't much of a thank-you, but it was something he could do.

CHAPTER SIX

"TORI, I'm sorry. Look at the time. I had no idea."

Tori straightened in her seat the following night and dropped her eyes to the computer's clock. How had four hours passed? One minute they were settling down to choose images and the next it was dark and Nathan's stomach had started vocalizing.

"Oh, wow. Me, neither. I got totally lost in the site."

She had. He'd used her images to start building a website that was elegant and clean, making stars of Fred and Wilma and building a simple text story around the two birds and the webcam. He did it in such a way that, later, when the birds bred, she'd be able to add their offspring easily. Tell a new generation of stories.

Though she had to admit he got visibly tense about the whole "future" part. Inexplicably.

But the moment passed and then so did the hours after it and now here they were, well after nine o'clock.

"Did you have plans?" she asked, mortified that some woman somewhere was tapping glossy acrylic nails on a counter top waiting for Nathan to appear.

"Nope." He finished a line of coding and turned to her, smiling with satisfaction. "You were my plans this evening."

That awkward pronouncement snapped her jaw shut audibly. She stared at him, speechless, a thick pleasure burbling upward.

I was?

"My goal was to finish this sucker tonight. A first draft, at least. No matter how long it took."

The broiling awareness thickened instantly to a hard, uncomfortable mass in her chest. He was going to stay up until all hours to get this project over with in the minimum amount of time. Her lips tightened. Of course he was. He had such a gift for making a girl feel *un*wanted.

"What if I'd had plans?" she asked, purely to be churlish.

His head came up. "Do you?"

No, but... "I might have."

He frowned at her prickly response. "Would you like me to go now? It's no problem."

Tori forced away the unexpected surge of defensiveness. She knew why he was here—the court order. Neither of them had pretended otherwise. Why the hell was she getting so offended by his haste? "No. Unless you want to? I'd understand."

It was ridiculous. Both of them stepping so carefully around the other's feelings.

Nathan chuckled first. "Let's start again." He sat up straighter. "Tori, it's late. Do you want to get some dinner?"

His smile melted her tension away to nothing. "Yes. Eating would be good."

"What do you like?"

"Anything but Portuguese chicken."

"What do you have against the Portuguese?"

"Nothing." She laughed. "Piri-Piri and I don't get along."

"I find it hard to imagine anyone or anything not getting along with you. You're very easy to be around."

More awkward silence. It was his color that rose this time, just slightly, in pinpricks high along his jaw. Tori scrabbled around for a distraction from just staring at him longer. "You wouldn't say that if you were with me right after I ingested Piri-Piri."

Oh, lord... The sort of thing you said around a campfire

after a long day climbing with your buddies, not around a hot man you couldn't stop staring at.

But Mr. Smooth took it in his stride. "Well, I've got a hankering for some Mexican. How about we clear our heads, take a walk and see if we can find somewhere with an outdoor table?"

Everything in her tightened up. She waved a carefully casual hand. "Why walk when we can dial? Eat in."

"Are you serious? We've been fixed in one position for four hours. We should probably be doing some yoga to unkink."

Immediately Tori thought of more collaborative ways of working the knots out of their muscles. A part of her longed to suggest it.

"Plus it's a beautiful night," he went on. "Come on, Tori, I'll take you to dinner. Somewhere with a view."

Again with the clenching muscles deep inside. What was going on with her? Was she really so out of touch with how this was done in normal circles? Not that anything was being done here tonight. This was just a practical necessity. They both had to eat.

"We've got one of the best views around right here," she said. "Why don't I set up the table on the roof while you pick up the takeout?"

The lines between his brows doubled. He shrugged. "Sure. Okay. Got any recommendations?"

Tori crossed to her fridge, relieved to be away from Nathan's scrutiny, and rifled through an enormous bundle of restaurant fliers pinned to its front.

"I should rephrase that," he said, deceptively light. "Any recommendations you *don't* have?"

She looked at the ridiculous wad in her hand and fought the bristle of discomfort at his gentle teasing. "I enjoy eating in."

"But not eating out?"

Her mouth dried up. She blinked at him urgently then stammered to speech. "W-wait till you've sat up there. You'll understand."

His eyes held hers while his brain ticked over. They nearly broiled with the intensity of his gaze. "You'd better make it special, then. Worth it."

And just like that it was a date.

What should have been a casual, convenient take-out meal had suddenly become a *special* tryst for two on the top of a New York building. He'd already seen the rooftop so she'd have to do more than just throw out a clean table cloth. And there was no electric light up there so they'd have to have candles.

Ugh...!

Not that a long-suppressed, girlie part of her wasn't thrilling at the idea of being on a date. After...how long? Even if it wasn't really a *date*-date. She hadn't sat across a dinner table from a man in five years. She wasn't even sure she remembered what people did on a date. Talked. Ate. Shared.

Kissed.

Her stomach flip-flopped. It was very telling that the idea of *sharing* with Nathan Archer was infinitely scarier than the idea of kissing him. Not that she'd given much thought to what it would be like to kiss him. Not truly. Okay, a few times...just casually wondering... Nothing serious.

Although now that the fantasy was in her head she had trouble shaking it.

"Yes." She thrust him the advertisement of the best TexMex in the area, just a few blocks over. "It'll be worth it."

Tori didn't take the word *special* any more lightly than the challenge she'd seen in Nathan's eyes as he headed out to buy the food. Whatever she did, she knew it had to be inspired.

Seven years ago she'd been hiking the Canadian Rockies and she'd had the best Mexican food she'd ever tasted in an Irish pub, of all places. They'd served sizzling meals on scorching hot tiles straight out of the fire, and margaritas in moonshine jars. Tonight she was desperate enough to recreate every part of that experience.

She'd loved it then, maybe Nathan would love it now.

She finished pouring margarita mix over a pitcher of hastily crushed ice, loaded up a couple of clean preserve jars and a crazy cowboy-hat candle her parents had sent her from Texas, and raced up the stairs. Then she came back down for the pizza stones she'd baked to blazing in her oven. She stacked them on top of each other and used the lifters to carry them carefully up the two flights of stairs. By the time she emerged, even her climbing arms were trembling from the strain.

She placed them carefully onto tiny terracotta blocks to protect the table. Then stood back to admire her handiwork.

Special. No denying it.

"Food's up," a deep voice said, behind her. She spun, still breathless from dashing around and kicking herself she hadn't dashed faster so she could have dedicated just sixty seconds to freshening up. So that, just once, he could see her at her best rather than her worst.

But then she remembered this wasn't a date-date. This was just dinner. "How did you get back in?"

"One of the perks of owning the building. I finally signed myself over a key."

Tori's heart fluttered. Just the idea that he could let himself in whenever he wanted… Was that uncertainty or excitement curling her stomach. Or was it just hunger?

She distracted herself with pouring slushy-ice margarita into the large empty jars while Nathan unloaded six containers of Mexico's finest. Then they both sat and got busy serving up rice, burritos, chili, tamales, stuffed peppers and skillet-fried fish onto their piping-hot stone tablets. The mouth-watering odors wafted around them. They loaded up their forks and sampled.

Nathan took a long, appreciative swallow from his moonshine jar to wash down the first mouthful of food and looked around before letting his contented eyes rest back on hers through the flicker of candlelight. "Okay, you win. This is without question the best way to eat Mexican *ever*."

Tori waved a hand. "I do it like this all the time."

"You do not," he laughed. Though he looked as if he'd have believed her if she said she really did. "When you didn't want to come with me I wondered if I'd done something to…" He frowned. "But this is great. I appreciate the effort you've gone to."

She knew she'd offended him by not going with him to dinner. Not that she could explain why when she didn't even know herself. She'd just been listening to her body. And her body said stay. "You're welcome. It is nice, huh?"

To illustrate the point she took a big swig from her moonshine jar. Then she bit into a piping-hot tamale. "Okay, wow. That's better than…"

"Than?"

The spicy heaven filled her mouth with excited juices. She rolled her eyes with pleasure. "Everything."

He lifted one sexy eyebrow. "Not everything, surely?"

She sat back in her seat and chewed a tamale appreciatively. "I'm struggling to think of something better."

Nathan selected one from the tray, trying for himself. "It is good," he nodded slowly then his mouth split into a heart-stopping grin. "But not that good."

Tori smiled to cover the sudden pounding of her heart. What she wouldn't give just to lean forward and wipe the tamale grease right off his lips…with her own. Slowly and thoroughly. Lingering on the bottom one. Her tongue slipped out onto her own lips in sympathy. "Well, you'd know, I guess!"

"Meaning?"

She stiffened her back. "Meaning I imagine you've had a lot of…everything…to compare to."

He smiled. "You're talking about sex."

Thump, thump… "No, *you* were talking about sex. I was talking about everything else."

His narrowed gaze saw too much. "But not sex?"

It had to come up sooner or later. "If these tamales are like sex then I can understand what all the fuss is about."

Nathan stared at her and she took another healthy swig of margarita then finally met his eyes silently.

His blazed back at her. "You've never had sex?"

"Try and contain your disbelief. It's insulting." Her words would have been, too, if she hadn't punctuated them by casually popping another tamale between her tingling lips and smiling. Way more casually than she felt.

He seemed to shake himself free of his stupor. "I'm sorry. I'm having a hard time believing it."

"Why?"

The blue in his gaze boiled as furiously as a hot spring. "Have you seen yourself, Tori?"

She shrugged. "Maybe my body is my temple?"

He put down his fork and leaned forward. "Come on. Seriously?"

"Why do people who've had sex always find it inconceivable that someone else hasn't?" And on what planet did she sit across the table from a relative stranger talking about her nonexistent sex life?

Planet Nathan, apparently.

He considered that in silence. "You're right. I just…" He shook his head. "How old are you?"

That question had only just occurred to him? She'd looked him up on the internet him almost immediately after she'd met him to find out the essentials. Which had seemed stupid at the time. "I'm twenty-six."

"Huh." He shook his head.

"You're really struggling with this." Amazing. And insanely flattering. Her whole body tightened in response. "I was one of the boys at prep school, then I spent most of my teen years in sports clubs." And why the heck was she defending herself so vigorously? "Then on the peaks I was just one of the boys again. Maybe I missed my window of opportunity."

"Uh, no, Tori, that window is still *wide* open for you."

She stared at him as his lashes blinked, apparently at half speed. Or was everything around her just happening sluggishly?

Certainly the blood in her veins and what air was in her lungs were thickening up dangerously.

"All those climbers, Tori. All that testosterone…"

The glow dissipated just a bit. "The last person in the world you want to climb with is someone you're emotionally involved with." She topped up her rice and got stuck into it, hoping to change the subject.

"Why?"

Hoping in vain. "It's like brain surgery. You should never do it on someone you love. Makes it hard to stay objective."

"You climbed with your brother."

The food in her mouth congealed into a tasteless paste. She chewed it carefully then took care swallowing so that it stayed down. "We had rules. To keep things separate."

Mostly.

"What kind of rules?"

"We'd climb in groups and always partner someone else. If we were climbing together we'd only do novice peaks." That was the rule. But the moment they set it, they'd started breaking it. Incrementally. Which could only lead to one thing…

"Defeats the purpose, I would have thought," Nathan said.

"Not many people get that." She looked at him differently in that moment, but then she remembered in his own industry he was the risk-taker. The first one to the highest peaks. "So we'd try for groups whenever we could so we could really climb."

"And no-one wanted to…get closer?"

Some of the taste in her food returned and she smiled gently. "With them, Rick was like a rottweiler on patrol. I think he'd heard too many of their stories."

"Ah. Big brothers."

"Physically, definitely. He out-muscled all of them. But I was older than him by fifteen minutes."

That stilled the fork halfway to his mouth. "You and Rick were twins?"

Her chest ached. Five years meant nothing to the ball of pain still resident in her chest. "We were the full cliché. Finishing each other's sentences, being sensitive to each other, sharing a house…" She felt the darkness hovering and took a deep breath to stave it off. "I even wore his clothes until puberty hit and he shot up four sizes. It drove him nuts."

"He was lucky to have you." Blue eyes held hers as he got used to that idea. A chili-like warmth spread through her body and added to the sluggish mix. "So that explains how you stayed under the radar until you were twenty-one. You haven't met anyone since you came to Manhattan?"

Tori's muscles coordinated to squeeze the last bit of oxygen from her lungs. Okay, when the conversation started working its way around to him it was definitely time to stop talking about sex. She forced a chuckle. "Mr. B's not really my type and Marco deCosta isn't old enough yet."

He laughed. "You think you're joking. The day will come when that kid's not going to be able to look at you without a cushion in his lap."

Tori spluttered, surprised by the unfamiliar sound of her own full belly laugh, and intrigued by the sudden forked frown lines that appeared between Nathan's brows. She saw a chance to learn more about him. She took it.

"Was there someone like that for you?"

Almost definitely. A man as simmering as Nathan didn't wake up one day and discover he'd become sexy. That kind of charisma came from childhood. And people responded to charisma. No matter the shape or size or age. They just changed the manner of response. He probably didn't even know he had it.

He blinked three times. Rapidly. "What?"

She glanced down at her empty margarita glass leaned forward to refill it, smiling more comfortably now that the topic had moved on. "If there was ever a candidate for a *Graduate* moment, it's you. Was there some kind of older woman that excited you, Nathan Archer?"

His gaze darkened and his mouth formed a harsh, straight line. Tension radiated from him in angry ripples.

"No."

That one word was sharp and tight and sounded like the ugliest of curses. And just like that, all the joy sucked out of their beautiful, special meal.

And both of them knew it.

"I..." What could she say? She let her lips fall shut and shifted her eyes away from the sudden strain. And chivalry must have died because Nathan didn't swoop in and try to ease her discomfort. He just sat there, as awkward as she was.

When he did finally speak his voice wasn't seductive any more.

"Why don't you have a job, Tori?" he nearly sneered. "How do you make rent?"

If she'd thought he was asking because he was interested, she would have told him, even though it was a critically rude question to ask. But he wasn't. He was asking to strike back at her for whatever she'd said to offend. So Nathan had a mean streak. Good to know. But she'd learned a thing or two about independence since moving to New York, and about how the world worked. Men like him might run the world but *she* ran her part of it.

She took her napkin and dabbed carefully at her lips, then pushed her chair away from the rooftop table. "Goodnight Nathan. I'll email you the web files and you can finish the site at your own apartment."

Her legs took her nearly all the way to the door before she felt his warm hand on her shoulder. She shrugged it off.

"Tori, wait." He moved around in front of her.

She crossed her arms in front of her. "Get out of my way, Nathan."

"Tori. I'm sorry. That was a cheap shot."

He wasn't moving, though. She kept her muscles rigid. "If you want me to listen to you then I suggest you get out from between me and the only way off this roof."

He glanced behind him and cursed under his breath, then stepped back. "I'm not making this better, am I?"

She turned her eyes up to him, taking care to keep them neutral. Suddenly she regretted the jar-and-a-half of margarita. She'd rather do this with a full complement of faculties. "I understand privacy, Nathan, better than most people. But if there's something you don't want to talk about, just say so."

He blew his frustration out through clenched teeth. "I let my guard down. I wasn't prepared. You blindsided me."

"With a casual question about your childhood?"

He looked as confused as she felt. "Everyone has triggers, Tori. You just stumbled onto one of mine. A raw one."

"So you hit back?"

His face fell and the abject misery glowed as neon as the storefronts down on the street. It niggled at her conscience. "That was my poor attempt at changing the subject. But it was harsher than I'd meant. I'm really sorry, Tori."

She stared at him a moment longer. "I pay the rent from money I got when I sold our house in Oregon."

He held up a hand. "It's none of my business. You were right not to—"

"I have nothing to hide, Nathan." Not, strictly speaking, true, but that was an inner demon for another lifetime. "Rick left me his half of our grandmother's house in his will. I sold it to come here and the rent comes straight out of that bank account. I don't even see it."

His shoulders slumped as he nodded and he wedged his hands into his jeans pockets. An eternity passed silently and then Tori turned for the door. Just as she reached for the handle, he spoke. Flat. Strained.

"I grew up in a building…much like this one."

The surprise was enough to halt her fingers on the door handle. But she didn't turn.

He continued behind her. "I know you imagined me growing up in a brownstone with loving parents and a matched pair of retrievers but that's not how it was."

His tension brought her focus around to him.

"Money was a rare commodity in my world. It was just

my mother and me and she was always…occupied…with her work."

Tori frowned at that choice of phrase.

"So, no…my childhood really wasn't peppered with idyllic moments, and the sorts of people in my mother's industry were hardly the type to inspire thoughts of great romance in a young boy."

"What people?" The pain was so evident as it twisted his handsome face into a fierce scowl, but she needed to understand. Even if her heart beat hard enough to hurt. "What industry?"

He lifted bleak eyes. "She was in sales."

Something about the way he said it. Like it was a lie he'd been telling for so long it had started to sound like the truth. She had to push the words out of her tight throat as a whisper. "What did she sell?"

A moment ago her heart had hammered because of him. Now it pounded blood ruthlessly against the walls of her arteries *for* him. Every part of her wanted to spare him from the truth she could read between the pained lines of his face.

Don't say it. Don't say it…

He shrugged. "Whatever men were buying."

Years of controlled breathing in oxygen-deficient environments had trained her well. She swallowed the shocked gasp. "She was a prostitute."

"At least."

She let that sink in. Imagining what he'd seen. Empathy for the hurt little boy he must have been flowed through her. "I'm sure she was only doing it to—"

"Don't." His hand shot up, large and firm. "Do you think it hurts less thinking she was doing it to feed and clothe and educate me? That belief tore my soul to shards until I realized it wasn't true. I gave up defending her years ago."

The sounds of carousing down on 126th Street drifted up to them in the silence that followed and mingled with the dense cloud of pain suddenly hanging heavy on her rooftop.

What should you say to someone who'd just spilled their

soul at your feet? Exposed their deepest secrets. Should you thank them for their trust? Should you comfort them for their shame? Should you gloss over it and try to put things back to how they were five minutes before and wish you'd been a little more tolerant and a lot less reactive?

Tori stepped up to him and curled her fingers around his and did the only thing she would have wanted in his place.

She traded him.

"Rick died while he was climbing with me," she said, quietly. "I watched him fall."

CHAPTER SEVEN

THAT brought his eyes up sharply and drove the misery straight from them. They filled instead with clear, glinting compassion. "You saw your brother die?"

"I watched every last second until I lost sight of him." *As penance.*

"Christ, Tori…"

"I don't want your pity, Nathan. Any more than you want mine. But I wanted you to know that I do understand something about triggers. About the everyday little things that leap up and ambush you when you're not at all prepared." *You blindsided me.* "And how hard it can be to stay rational when those feelings swell up."

They stared at each other until she finally spoke again. "So, I believe you when you say you're sorry. And when you say you didn't mean to be harsh. But can I trust you not to do it again?"

He was recovering his composure by the second. But he still frowned, not entirely back to cool, calm and collected Nathan. "You can trust me to not want to. And to do my very best not to let it happen again."

She stared at him, long and hard. Could she have offered more in his place?

Probably not.

"Good enough," she said, as a shudder rippled through her.

Nathan stripped off his coat and swung it around her bare

shoulders then held it together at her throat. The warmth soaked immediately into her frigid skin.

"You guys were climbing together?" he asked, carefully.

Of course he was going to ask. No one would walk away from a pronouncement like that. And she'd pressed *him* for details. But her instinctive defenses came straight into play and locked up her muscles.

"We broke our own rule."

"You were climbing alone." She nodded. As usual his quick mind took him straight to the important part. He freed a hand to rub up and down her arm. "You had to deal with it alone. That must have been hell."

No one had ever asked her this. Amongst the many, many questions about Rick's death at the inquiry, about which peak they'd chosen and why, about how thoroughly they'd hammered in the cams, no one had asked her what it had felt like walking off that mountain without the brother she adored. The boy she'd shared a womb with.

She dropped her eyes. "I couldn't leave him at all for the first few hours. But I couldn't drag him out either, he was too big. And I had to get back into radio range." She straightened her shoulders and snuggled more deeply into the warmth of Nathan's jacket. "Leaving him behind was the hardest thing I've ever done."

Third-hardest. Lying back against the snow drift knowing that she lived when he'd died…

Infinitely worse.

And number one…

She shook her head and blinked back the tears that always came when she relived that day. The last thing she wanted to do was cry in front of Nathan. She cleared her thick throat.

He pulled her toward him and wrapped his arms around his own coat, speaking against the top of her hair. "Would Rick blame you?"

Would he? Given they'd both ended up in the same perilous situation? That it could just as easily have been her on the wrong side of the anchor. "No. He hated it when I pulled rank. He considered us equals."

"Then let yourself off the hook. You didn't cause his death."

Her gut flipped back on itself and then squeezed into a tiny fist. There's no way he could truly understand, any more than she could do more than graze the surface of empathy for a little boy growing up in Nathan's impossible situation.

But in a weird, hopelessly antisocial way, knowing he'd endured pain too actually helped her manage hers. Knowing he understood—the concept if not the detail. It made her feel closer to him—to any human being—than she'd been in years.

She pressed her forehead against his shoulder.

"Thank you for telling me," he murmured, still against her hair. "I know it can't have been easy."

She leaned into his hard body where her fists clenched the front of his coat shut. *Honey, you don't know the half of it.* Watching Rick fall was only part of her nightmare. But there were some things you never aired.

Ever.

"You're welcome," she mumbled into his broad shoulder, letting herself enjoy the gift of his heat.

"We make quite a pair, huh?" His chuckle was more about tension than humor.

A pair. It took that phrase to draw her attention finally to something startlingly obvious that she'd been missing. She was standing under the stars, wrapped up snugly in Nathan's coat, buried in his arms with her lips practically pressed against his shoulder. Pairs made her think of couples. And couples made her think of coupl*ing*. And coupling made her think of…

Desire pooled thick and low in her body as his scent worked its way right into the pores of her skin and brought her mind full circle.

…*Nathan.*

Wrapped in the arms of the sexiest man she knew. Close enough that she could feel his steady heartbeat. Close enough that she could feel the plane of a ridged pectoral muscle beneath her clenched fists through his light sweater. Close enough that she could die right now and happily spend eternity swilling in his scent.

Time to move.

But no sooner did her body warn her to withdraw thaw those strong arms tightened. Keeping her close. One hand slid around to her back and recommenced its hypnotic circling there. Tori fought the insane desire just to melt into him. To surrender… everything…for a moment and let someone else take all the weight.

For a few heavenly moments.

How long had it been since anyone had touched her, let alone a man? Let alone like this. She took her moments of bliss where she could find them.

She leaned more closely into his hard body and added a fistful of his sweater into her tight clutch to keep them close. Her eyes drifted shut. Somewhere a thousand miles off music tumbled out of a window, the ballad drifting up to them on the night air. He leaned a fraction to his left and she followed him, loath to lose his warmth and the connection so soon. Then he moved back slightly to the right, that magic hand going around and around against her spine the whole time. And she followed.

Step…after step. Swaying left then right.

The rocking motion soothed as much as it serrated her body against his in a delicious, subtle, unfamiliar friction.

"Tori…" he mumbled, after a lifetime of gentle movement "…are we dancing?"

She didn't lift her lashes. The real world wasn't welcome back just yet. She mumbled, "No, we're shuffling."

She felt him smile against her forehead. "Okay, then."

They swayed in silence for the rest of the song. Nathan gathered her more firmly to him and Tori burrowed happily into his hold. She'd worked hard on her ability to push unwanted thoughts out of her head and she prayed thanks for it now, for the toasty, naive glow that could fill her soul while she kept the hard, real world carefully separate.

Their feet slowed to a halt and Nathan rubbed his face down hers, nudging it out and up, while his hands stayed tightly locked around her body. The seductive graze of his prickled jaw against hers, the blazing tangle of his breath and the hammer of his chest against hers…all whipped her heartbeat into riot and sent her senses skittering wildly around them like a mini dervish. A ton-weight pressed in on her chest.

Oh, God, he's going to kiss me…

And if he didn't, she was going to kiss him.

Or possibly die from oxygen deficiency.

She lifted her heavy lids and glanced at him. This close, his blue eyes were as clear and deep as any glacial lake but fringed by dark, soft lashes and blazing the icy fire of a question unasked. Somewhere in their depths a cautious uncertainty did a lazy backstroke but it was overwhelmed by the bubbling energy and focus of the last thing she'd ever expected to see from him.

Desire.

The moment their gazes met, all the reasons this was a bad idea—how unprofessional it was, why she didn't deserve a moment like this and why he was totally unsuitable and unsafe for her—dissolved just like her caution when she was facing a new mountain for the first time. Something other than sense was ruling play here, surging through her bloodstream and setting fire to every cell it passed. Bringing them scorching to vivid life.

Baying for more.

She let her mouth follow her eyes and turned her head naturally into the heat of his, dropping her lips slightly open.

His focus flicked down to them a bare moment before he closed the gap with a whispered groan.

The moment Tori's lips met Nathan's soft, warm ones, her body lurched with the involuntary gasp of air that rushed in. He captured her parted mouth with his again. He tasted of tangy citrus and chili and something rarer, something indefinable. Something she'd never experienced but wanted, in that moment, to keep forever. Her blood pounded everywhere it came close to the surface and robbed her of strength. Her mouth slid against his—tasting, exploring, feeding—and her hands curled more tightly into his sweater to keep him close. He shifted one hand lower, to press her hips into him and the other higher, tangling in her hair and taking the weight of her head as she let it fall back to give him more access.

"Tori…" he gasped, as they both sucked in a desperate breath. But she closed the gap again, nowhere near done with learning the shape of his lips, the taste of his mouth, and the slide of his teeth. He met her with interest, tangling tongues the moment she invited him in and sending her mind spinning off with sensation.

She curled one arm around his bent neck, pulling him closer, and his hand abandoned her nape in favor of a slow, sensual slide down her shoulder around to her side and under his own coat that heated her like a sauna all of a sudden. He burrowed under her thin cotton blouse and curved big fingers around her waist, his skin blazing hot against hers.

"So soft… So tiny…" he murmured against her mouth.

Funny, exactly the opposite of what she'd just been thinking. *So hard. So male.* The sort of man to make a tomboy feel like a princess. Alone together on this towering rooftop, under the magical stars. Where anything goes…

That thought brought her crashing back into focus. Back to the place where she didn't deserve the pleasure that was threatening to make her sigh. Back to the reality of who she was and who he was. And the fact they'd both got way too carried away with a margarita-fuelled candlelight dinner under the handful of stars that the lights of Manhattan allowed.

She gently pulled back out of his grasp. He let her go reluctantly, those big man hands trailing across her midriff as she stepped clear of him on unsteady legs.

Her chest heaved as hard as his as she breathed out a wobbly exclamation. "Wow."

He shook his disheveled hair. "You sure don't kiss like a novice, Tori."

Given she could count the number of men she'd kissed on one hand—fingers, not thumb—it definitely wasn't from practice. She took a shaky breath and smiled, filled for the first time with some ancient goddess magic that made her feel invincible. And woman. And utterly, utterly sensual.

"Natural aptitude?"

His laugh was as rocky as the geysers at Yellowstone, releasing the tension built up inside on a hiss. What did other people do in situations like this? When you'd just been crawling inside the skin of someone you were supposed to be working with? When you barely knew each other?

"Nathan, I—"

"Please don't say you're sorry, Tori. Let's just call it a great way to end a truly enjoyable evening."

"The evening's over?" Was that her voice sounding so thin? So disappointed?

"I…think it has to be. That conversation was only going one place and I'm not about to take you there."

Conversation? Well, they *were* using their mouths.

She probably should have been all uptight about the implication of Nathan's words. But she was too muddled to do anything but take him perfectly literally. "Why not?"

"Trust me. You deserve better."

"Than what? Dirty rooftop sex. Or dirty rooftop sex with you, specifically?"

He reached out and readjusted his coat more firmly around her shoulders, avoiding the question and accidentally brushing one still tingling breast as he slipped a button through its eyelet. It screamed at her to argue the point.

"When you have sex for the first time Tori, it should be memorable for all the right reasons."

Will you be there, Nathan? But she couldn't ask that. Her courage only went so far.

He smoothed the sleeves of the coat down her arms and the move struck her as just a little bit too patronizing. It plucked away more of the golden strands that had lain so heavily over her usual defenses. Her eyes narrowed. "Shouldn't that be my decision?"

He stared at her and ran well-manicured fingers through his own hair to restore some order. "Tell you what, Tori. Tomorrow morning when you no longer have a belly full of Mexican food and margarita and lust, if you still think this is a good idea you just give me a call and I'll happily oblige. But tonight…it's goodnight."

Oblige. Like it would be some kind of civic duty. Part of his community service. Anger bubbled up. "What makes you think I don't have plans tomorrow?"

Wow, did rampant sexual frustration make everyone this irritable?

But it seemed to be catching. "You haven't had a single plan since I met you," he gritted.

That was too close to the truth, and she felt the boiling of sudden shame. To a man like him, staying at home a lot probably did seem like loser territory. Let alone all the time. She used the moments it took to shrug off his coat to master her brewing pique, and then folded the jacket carefully before handing it back to him.

She met his frown and threw him her best couldn't-care-less smile. "Don't wait by the phone, Nathan. If it rings it won't be me."

CHAPTER EIGHT

THE phone did ring the following workday—many times—and it was never Tori.

Nathan stared up gridlocked Columbus Avenue toward Morningside. Again.

She'd said she wouldn't call. She would have come to her senses five minutes after coming down from that rooftop—from the amazing natural high of their kissing. Women like Viktoria Morfitt didn't belong with men like him. No matter how much tequila they'd ingested. She came from a good, wholesome family and he…just didn't.

But she'd know that now. After his extraordinary Dr. Phil full-confession moment by the stairs.

What the hell had he been thinking? No one but his most trusted circle knew about his mother. Dean and his parents, his school counselor who'd endorsed him for early admission, the financial aid registrar.

Okay so a few people knew. But he'd never imagined Tori would be one of them. And at his own admission. Desperate times, desperate measures—the way she'd stalked, so stiff-backed from the table. It had just tumbled from his lips rather than lose her and the beautiful evening she'd gone to such trouble to create. He would have said just about anything in that moment to keep her with him.

And then she'd trumped it. Well and truly.

She was there when her brother died. The *only* person there.

What kind of courage did it take to go for help and hold it all together until rescue arrived? Half a day on a mountain with a corpse that, just hours before, was the person you'd loved and teased and spent a life with.

Unimaginable.

But she'd endured it. Her eccentricities made a little bit more sense of that now. Something like that was bound to mess with your head. Change your priorities and the way you approached life. Even her folks had opted out and hit the road. Maybe this crazy existence she was living was the Tori equivalent of turning nomad.

Between the origami laundry, the tutoring, the crazy-dog minding, the photographs and the falcons—and there was undoubtedly a stack of things she was doing that he wasn't aware of—it was just as well Tori didn't have a job to be going to. She'd never have the time. She hadn't liked it when he rattled her about having no plans, but facts were facts. She was always home when he called, she was always home when he came for community service or when he dropped by with camera parts or televisions. As if she truly had nowhere else to be.

He frowned. Nor, apparently, did he.

An honest-to-goodness, New-York's-richest-list bachelor, struggling to find something better to do with his time than visit a beat-up century-old building uptown.

It wasn't until that moment—until he started counting up the visits—that he realized how much time he was spending at Tori's or on the phone to Tori. Or hunting down the perfect replacement apartment for Tori. Or thinking about Tori. Very little of it could be chalked up to a court order. There was something about her. Something unusually comfortable about being with her. Amazing when you consider how very *un*comfortable he was in that building. Yet here he was trying to come up with a good reason to go back, even now.

He glanced at his desk. And here he was finalizing the documents that would tumble the building to the ground. Even as he'd sat on the roof of it and eaten Mexican and kissed one of its inhabitants.

Guilt chewed like a dog on the rawhide of his conscience, but then reason kicked in. It was fine; Dean's team had already located alternative lease accommodation for twenty-eight of the thirty-five tenants—dog-friendly ones, kid-friendly ones, nana-friendly ones—and the remaining nine weren't far off being finalized. All within a twenty-block radius of the existing building or the tenants' workplaces. All with longish leases to give them time to make their own alternative arrangements. To see them right. He had something special in mind for Tori. Bigger and more comfortable than her modest little Morningside rental.

The phone rang and he reached for it absently. "Archer."

"I'm calling to apologise."

He dropped into his chair and then stood again—ridiculously—at the sound of Tori's breathless voice. For one crazy moment he thought she might be taking him up on his offer, tacky and ill-conceived as it had been. The absolute last thing he wanted to do was complicate things further by getting physical. Even if it was also the thing he wanted most.

But if he wanted to touch her, he'd have to tell her what was going on. About the demolition.

"Apologise for what?"

"I was supremely ungrateful last night. I never thanked you for all the work you did on the website. I was just looking at it again on my desktop. It really is amazing."

Apology accepted. As if he wouldn't. "Just a bit more to do and it will be ready to go."

"Thank you, Nathan."

God, he loved the way she said his name. That gentle west-coast accent, the breathlessness like light fingers trailing down his spine or the touch of her lips.

"And I wanted to make good on my part of the trade, at last," she went on.

Uh-oh...

"So I thought I could throw a small open house to celebrate the peregrine website going live. Give you a chance to meet some of your tenants. Give me a chance to get them excited about Wilma and Fred."

From her point of view it was a good idea to get the other tenants invested in her falcons. But it was a spectacularly bad one from his, for so many reasons. He still wasn't in a crashing hurry to meet anyone else from the building—anyone who might recognize him, or might see Darlene in Nathan's own dark coloring and do the math. Or simply recognize his surname. He had no idea how many of them had known his mother by anything other than her working name.

And somehow he thought it might be easier for them as tenants not to have met the man who was about to rehome them. To have shared coffee and cake with them, unawares. That felt more than a little wrong.

Like keeping the truth from Tori was starting to.

"So I was wondering if you could give me a realistic time frame on go-live day?"

Realistically? Today, if he pulled his finger out and got working on it instead of sitting around mooching about her. But the moment the website went live he'd have no more falcon project to work on and no more reason to see Tori.

And he really wanted to see her face when he showed her the new apartment. Personally. Frame by beautiful frame.

"Uh, how does Friday sound?"

"Friday would be great. That gives me a few days to plan. Will I—" she cleared her throat and spoke in a rush of words "—will you be coming around before then?"

"I have the code on my flash drive, so I can finish it here if you like. And I can do all the uploading and testing remotely." He paused, wondering if he was laying it on too thick when he really only wanted to know one thing. "I wasn't sure I'd be welcome."

Her sigh breathed down the phone. "I'm so sorry for

being snappish, Nathan. You didn't deserve that. We're both consenting adults. And it was just a kiss."

"Right..."

She didn't sound any more convinced about that than he did, but her remorse seemed entirely genuine. And, who knows, if she was as inexperienced as she made out then an unplanned, hot-and-heavy make-out session might have thrown her equilibrium. It threw his and he was much more used to casual contact. He specialized in casual. "Tensions were high. I imagine we both said more than we meant to."

"I guess it wasn't the usual after-dinner conversation," she murmured.

Hardly.

Dead brother. Hooker mother. *Another mint?*

"Tell you what. I'll finish the site from here and bring it round to you tomorrow evening. Will you be home?" It was almost pointless asking, but assuming—with her—would be relationship suicide.

He frowned. Relationship? Was that what they had? He didn't really do relationships, not with women. He saved those for the diminishing circle of friends he trusted. Relationships required emotional investment. Sex required nothing but time.

Why did he even care what she thought of him? But his body's response to the soft, low smile in her voice as she said, "Yes, I'll be home," made him realize he was starting to care. Inexplicably. And very much.

And that really wasn't a good idea.

She might be the virgin in a technical sense, but when it came to genuine, loving relationships she was miles ahead of him. She'd had a brother she'd loved with everything in her. Loving parents. Grandparents.

He simply had no point of reference at all.

When it came to love *he* was the virgin.

He shoved his hands deep into his trouser pockets. This really couldn't be about what he wanted. If it was he'd just call

Simon around to the front, get him to drop him at Morningside and not collect him until morning.

As he had so many times in so many other buildings in the city.

But Tori was different. He was drawn to her in a way he could barely understand.

Deep inside. Where he never, ever went.

Time to set up some boundaries.

"They have eggs!"

Tori launched herself at Nathan the moment he stepped through her door, her excitement driving away the residual discomfort at what a social klutz she had been two nights ago. Sure, it had been a while between kisses—a long while—but that was hardly Nathan's fault, hopefully he'd forgive her ridiculous overreaction. Her embarrassing and far too revealing *over-participation* in the kiss.

Or not, she realized, as he gently but firmly peeled her arms off him and set her away, keeping his focus safely elsewhere. A part of her wanted to shrivel at the careful neutrality of his expression, but the thrill surging like champagne bubbles through her blood couldn't care less about her blushes, and so she snagged his hand and dragged him to the television where the webcam showed a fabulous center-of-screen view of Wilma happily spread low in the nest box, patiently guarding something.

That got his attention. "Have you seen the eggs?" he asked.

"Nope. But she wouldn't be brooding if they weren't there." A strange, almost forgotten lightness filled her. It had been a long time between lightnesses, too. She turned her face up to him. "They've bred, Nathan!"

He wasn't looking at the screen anymore; his eyes were fixed firmly on her. And they were dark with something she thought was confusion. Or surprise. Or both. "You're radiant."

Heat raced into her cheeks. She'd made an effort to dress for him this time. Nothing flash, just her best, butt-hugging jeans and a simple shirt in the most flattering color she owned. She knew she had no real right to be this happy, but Nathan just noticing when she looked good added to her already erupting excitement about the falcons. "I'm sure it's not *that* unusual. I can be happy."

The expression settled into a frown. "It's good to see."

But then his focus flicked back to Wilma who looked comically uncertain about what her instincts were making her do. The she-falcon glanced anxiously around her, as if expecting more. Or some help. Tori hugged her arms around herself and worked hard not to bounce up and down.

Babies. Not the first she'd seen, but definitely the first she'd gone all squishy over.

"How long before the eggs hatch?" Beside her, Nathan's voice was measured but pleasingly rumbly.

"About a month."

"Then what happens?"

"Then Wilma and Fred raise the ones that survive. Teach them how to fly, hunt. How to be independent."

"How long does that take—until they're independent?"

Was he worried he wouldn't be around to see it? "About six weeks. You can watch it all on the webcam, Nathan."

Something finally dented the natural high she'd been on since switching on the webcam and seeing Wilma on the nest. Heck, since she'd drowned in Nathan's kiss on the rooftop. How sad that he wouldn't be here to see the hatching in person. That they'd go their separate ways any day now.

Sad for him.

Sadder for her.

Her heart squeezed hard. "We have to get this live as soon as possible," she mumbled, thrown by the sudden, intense ache. "People will want to see this part. How much time do you have this afternoon?"

His enigmatic eyes came back to hers, distracted by a visible uncertainty but then clearing as he seemed to make a decision. Their warmth reached out to her. "As much as you need."

Tuesday—Nathan had to be busy with work stuff today. No wonder he was distracted. The time he was giving her was so generous.

She took a deep breath.

"Well then, let's get to work."

They spent the whole afternoon and most of the night editing footage from the moment the webcam was powered up, hunting in fast forward for the best bits of footage and making a "What You Missed" archive for the website: Wilma and Fred checking out the box, visiting and revisiting, a short, solitary, X-rated Wilma and Fred, and then, finally, Mom on the nest and Dad hovering anxiously by, alert for interlopers.

If Tori had stuck her head out that bathroom window they would have been off, never to return. No question.

Wilma had laid during the night so it was almost impossible to see how many eggs there were, but peregrines usually produced three or four with the hope that at least one would survive to juvenile status. She'd have to feed eventually so perhaps there'd be a brief moment when Fred took over when Tori could catch a glimpse of how many eggs they'd made together. Would there be a Pebbles and BamBam, too?

She sighed. *Ah, reproduction, such a wonderful thing.*

And not just because she couldn't get her mind off the human equivalent lately; it was such a disturbingly short mental journey from Nathan to babies.

They worked through dinner, sharing ideas, compromising on differences, anticipating each other's thoughts, and celebrating the amazing footage and photos that the site brought together. Tori caught herself resting her gaze more on Nathan than the screen several times and had to force her focus back to proofreading the text content or making a decision on footage, only to catch herself doing it again a few minutes later.

He compelled her gaze toward him exactly the way her

climbing tools sometimes stuck to the natural magnetism of certain rock faces.

His own fault for being so good to look at. He was tall and built for endurance, where her climbing friends had been solid and built for bursts of massive full-body power, but she would have picked Nathan anyway. His brilliant mind would have ensnared her even amongst all their outdoorsy muscle. But the thickening stubble of beard he hadn't shaved off since Sunday night grew hard along his strong cheekbones and highlighted their strength. And she was way too aware of how his lips had felt on hers to worry whether they might be, technically, a little on the thin side by Hollywood standards. And every time she had an idea that he didn't like and he slid those deep-blue eyes sexily sideways at her in doubt…she just melted that little bit more.

She stared at him now, while his attention was thoroughly focused on the computer screen.

It couldn't hurt just to look, surely. To speculate.

All the excitement she felt now about the peregrine eggs only simmered in amongst the residual tingles from spending the last two nights reliving the feel of his mouth on hers. The strength of his arms pinning her to him. The feel of his hard planes under her hands. And creating endless, breathless scenarios about what would have happened if she hadn't pulled away from him back on the rooftop. If she'd heeded the raw, base call of a virile male. If she'd let the hungry ancient goddess in her respond.

Knowing how much she needed that.

Believing how little she deserved it.

"Coffee?"

She was on her feet and moving towards the kitchen before he could answer. She gulped down a glass of cold water and willed away the pheromones she could practically smell churning around her. They weren't helping her keep her mind on the job and the last thing she wanted was to be sitting so close to Nathan while practically radiating "take-me-now" vibes.

Rick had lost the chance of finding the right person for him; reaching out and grabbing what Nathan offered just didn't sit right with her.

Not that Nate had really offered anything. Nothing serious, anyway. Sex…if she wanted it. His offer to *oblige* might have been flippantly delivered, but Tori had the feeling that if she took him up on it he'd be as good as his word. And hopefully every bit as good as her fantasies. But that's it. A Manhattan-born captain of industry just didn't do more than slum it with maladjusted girls from Morningside.

Cinderella never would have actually ended up with the prince.

But she'd have had fun trying.

Tori dug down deep into her conscience to see how it felt about that? About a strictly physical experience. Exploring these feelings she'd pretty much given up on ever having. Not romance, not love—definitely not happy ever after—those were totally out of bounds. Just happy ever…now. A little more lightness now that she'd been reminded of how good it felt. She held her breath better to hear her conscience's verdict.

Silence. Just the relentless thump of her tortured pulse. And that was as good as a yes.

She lifted her head and blazed molten fire at the broad back of the man in her living room. The reality of what to do next was almost crippling. She'd never seduced anyone in her life. Of those few paltry kisses she'd had, she'd only instigated one and that was stolen from a very unwilling Michael Toledo in fourth grade and it hadn't really ended all that well. He'd cried and she'd spent the afternoon in the Assistant Principal's office sharpening pencils.

The idea of walking up to Nathan and grabbing his square chin the way she'd done with Michael's round, pudgy one…

Not an option.

But neither was backing away from this decision now that she'd made it. Now that her conscience had, amazingly, approved. It was far too rare a gift to give back.

"Have you got something stronger than coffee in that kitchen, Tori?" he asked, lightly, back over his shoulder.

If I had, I'd be drinking it right now. Heat simmered up from under her shirt as her whole body got in on the act of wanting him.

"Uh…no. Why?"

He turned and smiled one of his most knock out smiles. "Because unless there's anything new you've thought of, then we are officially done."

That stopped her cold. Every part of her.

The heat…

Her pulse…

Her tight breath.

Like the water sucking out to sea in advance of a tidal surge. If they truly were done, he had no good reason to be here anymore. The wave crashed back in over all the flipping fish of her emotions, carrying blind panic at the thought she wouldn't see him again.

Her voice shook as she risked speech. "The website's finished?"

"Yep. It'll take about three minutes to upload all the files and then your falcons are out there for the world to see."

Excitement and terror scrabbled and clawed for dominance. She'd been looking forward to this moment since Nathan had first put the idea of a webcam into her head. But for it to come now—just when she'd decided to throw herself at his feet…

Three minutes. That wasn't a lot of time for finesse.

She crossed out of the kitchen and moved towards him with purpose. "I've changed my mind."

He frowned at her. "You don't want to go live?"

Why hadn't she worn something more alluring than jeans and a T-shirt? Or brushed her teeth before answering the door? "I do want to go live. I've changed my mind about…" *Oh, God.* Her heart pounded hard enough to hear in her voice. "…about our conversation on Sunday night."

A cautious suspicion blinked to life in his eyes. "Which one?"

"The one in which you said you'd sleep with me if I still wanted to in the morning."

All six-foot-three of crafted muscle stiffened instantly. "Ah, Tori..."

She stepped up closer to him, hard against him and did her best to saturate her voice with confidence. "I still want to."

He slid his hands up her arms, but not to bring her closer. He forced an inch of sanity between them. "No, you don't. You're just excited the project's finished."

She used her upper-body strength to resist his gentle pressure. "I am excited that the website's finished, but not that our time together will be finished."

And there it was. Couldn't be plainer than that.

Take me, I'm yours.

He groaned and his tongue stole out to wet suddenly dry lips. Tori's eyes locked on it the way Fred and Wilma tracked pigeons. "Tori... You have terrible timing."

"Why?"

He looked around for inspiration. "It's 2:00 a.m. We've worked into the night."

Desperate measures. Nathan might be in denial, but she knew exactly what she wanted—for the first time in years. She slid one hand boldly under his shirt and rested it right over the hard warmth of his heart. It thumped powerfully against her fingers and he flinched backward on another deep groan.

She smiled to see him so affected. "I may not have been born in New York, but I'm pretty sure even here 2:00 a.m. is a perfectly good time for..."

The actual words evaporated.

"Sex?" His expression softened and he cupped his hands around hers through his fine shirt "You can't even say it comfortably—how were you planning on doing it?"

Heat roared up her neck. "I was hoping there wouldn't be

a whole lot of talking about it. I certainly wasn't expecting to have to beg."

She glanced away, but his silence brought her eyes back to him. "You wouldn't need to beg, Tori. I meant what I said the other night." His eyes flicked to the bedroom. "I would like nothing more than to carry you in there right now."

"Then *oblige* me." She threw the word intentionally back at him, her chest heaving.

He winced. "It wouldn't be fair on you, Tori. I can't offer you more than a good time."

"Okay." That tied in nicely with her own needs, anyway.

"It's not okay. You deserve someone who can care for you. Who can give you…more."

"I'm not asking for more."

He stroked her cheek with one finger. "You should be. You're worth someone's whole heart."

Rejection flamed wildly beneath her blood, whipping it into a bubbling frenzy. "Apparently not yours."

His lips tightened. "I should go."

If he went he wouldn't be back. She scrabbled for inspiration as he started to push away. "I'm asking you to be with me, Nathan. To teach me."

He swore under his breath and lifted pained blue eyes back to her. She wedged herself bodily into the chink she could suddenly see in his armor. He wanted to do this. He *did* want it. "Are you seriously going to walk away and leave me wondering?"

His gaze narrowed. "Wondering what?"

"How we'd be together."

His nostrils flared and his lips pressed together against something he wanted to say. His voice vibrated with tension when he said instead "You'll meet someone else." But he flinched slightly as he said those words and Tori's chin—and confidence—lifted.

She tossed her hair back. "You'd prefer to outsource this?"

Deep heat blazed dark and raw in his eyes, turning them

indigo. *No.* Everything in him said it. But outwardly he just repeated "I should go."

He swung around and checked the files had finished uploading, grabbed his coat and turned for the door. "Goodbye, Tori. I'll call in a few days and see how the site's going."

No!

Him leaving now was not an option. Not when she knew full well she'd never see him again. Not when she knew he wanted her as much as she wanted him.

"Nathan—"

He was out in the hall before she could pull enough salient words together. She shot out after him. "I'll ride down with you."

He didn't exactly protest, but he strode down the hall and into the stairwell without a word. His whole body was rigid as his long legs carried him down the stairs. She kept up easily, and her light jog matched her fevered thoughts perfectly. Neither of them spoke as they emerged onto the eighth floor. She noticed his glance didn't flick toward the empty 8B the way it usually did, then he palmed the elevator button.

The elevator car was still sitting at the top of its range and when the doors opened, she slipped in behind him and then stood in the same stony silence as him and stared at the faded light countdown that marked their interminable descent.

Confusion and mortification swirled in her addled mind.

He was really going to walk away from this! From her. Despite wanting her as much as she wanted him. The incredible buoyancy she'd been increasingly feeling since he'd turned up on her doorstep, court order in hand, came into crashing context.

He made her feel good. *He* brought lightness back into her world. *He* had her springing out of bed in the morning rather than crawling.

Nathan.

Not just any guy. And not just because he was good-looking. And not just because he was charming.

Because she was falling for him.

And as the momentousness of that sank like a stone into the pit of her stomach, Tori knew she was finished begging. Because him saying no now would mean so much more than him saying no five minutes ago, before she realized her heart was involved—the heart that was hammering hard enough to burst right open. But she couldn't just let him walk. Even if he was only in this for the short term.

She couldn't keep him forever—fine—but couldn't she have him for just a bit longer?

The elevator lurched to a halt on the ground floor and the old door started to groan open. *Only seconds now...*Nathan reached across to slide back the ornate outer door opening into the building's entry foyer. The move brought him closer to her for a bare moment and she swayed toward him instinctively. But then she squared her shoulders, lifted her eyes and spoke quietly past her wildly thumping pulse.

Not a plea, just a fact.

"Last chance, Nathan."

The corner of his eye twitched and his jaw tightened, but otherwise he kept his focus fixed on the door to the street—his escape—then stepped past her out the elevator door, and into the silent lobby...

...and was gone.

The acid of rejection burned high in her throat as the doors retracted agonizingly slowly across the elevator opening. Old, familiar pain burbled up from the place she'd worked so hard to bind it.

She should have known. Her conscience had set her up so thoroughly for this lesson in payback. It had seen what she, clearly, had not. That despite the dubious romance of a tequila-fuelled kiss, Nathan really wasn't all that interested in more from her. Not even casually. No matter what he said.

She kept her focus forward, her chin high until the moment the doors obscured her from his view should he look back.

But the second she couldn't see him—nor he, her—she

released the pain in a choked moan. She'd survived much worse, she knew she would survive this. But in that very moment it was impossible to imagine how.

Suddenly the door's slide yanked to a halt, and Tori lifted her face as it hauled open with more gusto than it had ever displayed, and Nathan surged back into the elevator. He swept her up in his tide and pushed her back against the rear of the tiny box, his mouth crushing down on hers while she was still sucking in an elated breath.

"This doesn't mean I care for you." He ground out the words against her lips.

Triumph exploded in every cell of her body. Her arms hooked instantly around his strong neck, her hands plunging their way deep into his dark hair, and she breathed a response in the half heartbeat he took to get a better angle on her mouth. "I don't want you to care for me."

God help her, it was the truth. And also the worst of lies.

Recognizing the truth was so exquisitely painful it was hard to separate it from the elation still surging through her blood. She didn't deserve someone like Nathan in her life forever. The only thing letting her have this moment for herself was the fact that there was no chance of it ending well for her beyond the priceless opportunity to feel this glorious man naked up against her. To steal something to remember him by. To remember lightness by—for when it was gone again.

He'd been crystal-clear. For now, not forever.

No wonder her conscience had been fine with it. It saw what a dead end lay ahead. It had nothing to lose.

Nathan groaned against her mouth and shuffled her sideways so that he could punch the up button on the elevator. She lurched against him as it began its creaking ascent, but he held on to her, sharing air, tangling tongues, grinding into her, their body temperatures rising with the elevator. Tori grew lightheaded from oxygen depletion and plain old sagging relief and she clung to him desperately.

There was a feverish quality to Nathan's kisses that hadn't

been there on the rooftop. An urgency that perfectly matched her own. He leaned her against the left side of the elevator and then a moment later pulled her back up into the centre, before shifting to the right. Every time they moved a different part of her throbbed with need, but no part of her was going to get satisfaction.

He was as restless as his hands…and as unsettled as she was beginning to feel. She tore her mouth free and gasped "What's wrong?"

His gaze ricocheted around the tiny space, hyper. "Nothing."

Tori frowned. She could be self-conscious, she could worry that he'd changed his mind or that she'd done something wrong. But something about the wild passion on his face as he'd forced his way back into her elevator forced the doubt to heel. This wasn't about her. And the fact it was about him worried her even more.

That was pain she could see in the shadows at the back of his eyes.

The elevator continued its torturous ascent, grumbling unhappily. She pulled her fingers out of his hair and slid them to either side of his flushed face, forcing him to look at her, and held his eyes steadily.

If he changed his mind now her life would be over, but at least she would know.

She stroked his jaw with her thumb. "Tell me."

Heat pumped off him and the wildness of his eyes took a moment to ease. Emotion flickered across his face until it finally resolved, taking the frown lines with it.

"Nothing's wrong." He took a deep breath and drank her in. Really looked at her. "Just a memory." A tiny smile broke free and he stooped to kiss her gently. "Something that doesn't belong here anymore."

He kissed her again—a different kind of kiss to his first ones, to the rooftop. It was a kiss full of light. Full of relief. She stretched up and kissed him back, taking care to strip it of any clue about how deeply her heart was involved. It was still a good kiss. Actually it was a fantastic kiss.

Which only made her wonder what it would be like to kiss him with love between them. Instead of…

Whatever it was they had.

The elevator hit the end of its reach and Tori led the way out to the stairwell, her heart hammering relentlessly against her ribs.

He must have picked up on her tension because he said, "You're sure?"

She stopped and looked back at him in the entry to the dim stairwell. One strong arm stretched up the door frame, hovering on the cusp between common sense and no return, equally willing to go with either. His concerned frown only drew her more to him.

"You thought I wouldn't be?" she murmured.

"You know what this is—between us?"

She thought about that long and hard. "I have no idea what this is. But I don't require promises, Nathan. Only honesty. I'm in no position to be asking for forever."

This might be as close to forever as she came.

She held out her hand towards him, steadier and more confident than she felt, and he pushed himself away from the door frame and was with her in a few easy steps, his eyes holding hers. His fingers dwarfed hers, stroking softly across her skin, and then folding through her own to form a sensual lifeline.

She led the way up two flights of stairs toward her bedroom—the one room he'd not been into—and gripped that human lifeline as tightly as any mountain rigging.

CHAPTER NINE

RIGHT up until the moment the cool of her bed linen kissed her naked back, Tori might have chickened out. But the moment she'd felt the touch of the safest *place* in the world within the safest *part* of her world in the arms of the safest *man* in her world, she knew this was one hundred-percent right. It wasn't forever—they both knew that—but it had been coming since the first moment she saw him.

Nathan's lips hadn't left hers since the two of them crashed through her new door, twisted up in each other's arms, stumbling in their rush to get each other naked. To know each other. To love each other.

Just for one night.

Now, his skin still radiated a blazing heat, lying half-sprawled on top of her, one sweaty leg thrown over her two, simmering blue holding her enraptured while her strained chest rose and fell heavily from the gymnastics of the past hour.

Of all the things she had secretly hoped to discover about making love for the first time—all the things she *did* discover—finding out she almost wasn't fit enough was not on her expected list.

"My chest is about to explode," she gasped. "You'd think being climbing-fit would have helped. How do normal people cope?"

Nathan chuckled close to her ear as his fingers traced lazily over the ridges of her brow, her nose, her lips. She bit gently at the fingers and heard the controlled heaving of his own lungs between his words. "I'm not sure most 'normal' people would have put quite that much effort into it."

Tori's flushed skin couldn't accommodate any more blood, so her blush had no purpose. "Really? Was I too…?"

Vigorous? Enthusiastic? *Trying too hard?*

Nathan's lips split wide in a dirty grin. "You were amazing." Then the smile sobered just slightly and he dragged his thumb over her bottom lip. "You *are* amazing."

Oh...

Moments like that made it hard to forget this was a one-off.

Moments like the one when he'd turned her blazing gaze to his and held it. When he'd gently stroked away the sneak of moisture that had escaped her eye after it all got too overwhelming. When he'd pulled her into his shoulder and murmured words of reassurance as she'd fragmented into a million shards of the sweetest diamond dust.

He hadn't made love to her like a man who didn't care.

And she hadn't responded like a woman who didn't want to be cared for.

Whoops on both their parts.

Not that there was any question about *whether* she cared. She wouldn't have risked—trusted—just anyone. Only Nathan. Arrogant, brave, wounded Nathan. But would she ever lie in her big bed again and not think of the wasted size of it? Would she ever touch her lips and not taste him there? Would she ever be the same? There were some consequences that a condom couldn't prevent.

The emotional ones.

Maybe she shouldn't have given in to her baser instincts and ripped open Pandora's box knowing she would never let herself keep what she found inside.

Not that he was offering. At all.

Even now.

Her eyes slid sideways again and collided with his electric-blue one. "Thank you, Nathan."

"This wasn't charity, Tori." His large hand slid around to tangle in her damp hair. "I've wanted to get you naked since the day you ratted me out to the cops."

She smiled. Was that only three weeks ago? "I'm still grateful. I'll always remember this."

When you're gone.

Nathan wiggled in harder against her and buried his lips somewhere near her ear. She was just as happy not to see that thought echoed back to her in his gaze. Her lashes drifted shut as his lips traced the outline of one lobe and she groaned her appreciation. As tired as she was it was a strange kind of exhaustion. The kind that could leave you ready for a repeat almost immediately. Not a bad system, really.

"There's still the launch party, remember?" he murmured, hot and damp against her ear.

Her eyes flew open. She spoke to the ceiling, virtually holding her breath. "You're going to come?"

"I figure I owe it to Wilma and Fred for invading their privacy so thoroughly yesterday."

Thoughts of the brief, frantic bird-sex they'd caught on the camera brought a smile to her lips. "Maybe they returned the favor just now."

He lifted his dark shaggy head and turned towards the window. Neither of them had bothered with the curtains so the whole bedroom stood exposed to the darkened ledge outside. The bed shook as Nathan laughed, deep and sexy.

It felt way too good to lie naked in his arms joking around. Dangerously comfortable.

Dangerously addictive.

She forced her thoughts onto something else. "I'm not sure how many people I should invite. It's not that big an apartment."

Beside her Nathan stilled. She could practically hear him thinking. Finally he spoke. "You'd like a bigger place?"

"Not especially, though it would be handy at a time like this." Not that throwing a party happened more than once every… five years. In fact, this would be her first.

Actually, a crazy dream of renting the apartment next door with its park-facing aspect and opening it up into one big apartment had occurred to her last year. Not that it was available, and not that she could afford it if it was.

Nathan rolled onto his back, dragging the light covers up and over both of them. He turned toward her on the pillow. "If you had a blank check, what improvements would you make?"

She frowned at him. "Is all post-coital conversation this suburban?"

He leaned over and kissed her—roughly, soundly. Fabulously. "I'm recharging. Humor me."

Tori's heart squeezed. After what they'd just done together how could a simple kiss still steal her breath? Yet it did.

"Ah, blank check…okay," she said as soon as she was able. "I guess I wouldn't mind making it a bit bigger. And actual park views instead of the glimpse I get right now. But I wouldn't want anything flash."

"Why not?"

Because there was something suitably monastic about living a simple life. Denying herself comforts. "I don't need it."

"You don't need a tantalizing Mexican spread on a rooftop either but you enjoyed it."

She had—a slip on her part. Maybe she'd become all-round too indulgent since meeting Nathan Archer.

He took her silence as reluctance and nudged her with his foot. "If you won't take pleasures, then what about conveniences?"

He really wanted to play this game. Okay. She turned to face him. "I guess a built-in laundry would be convenient. It would save me having to go to the basement."

"Balcony?"

She expelled a frustrated outburst on a small puff. "If we're going to totally redesign the building, sure!"

"Not here then. Anywhere. Anywhere in Manhattan."

She sat up straighter and threw him her best probing look. "Are you trying to seduce me with imagined spoils? Because… you know…I'm already naked, you really don't have to try that hard."

His smile turned sideways to fit her mouth better and he kissed her to silence. "Come on, Tori," he said when they finally came up for air. "Play the game. Anywhere at all on Manhattan."

Her eyes explored the room as though she'd find inspiration there. "Okay…if imaginary money truly is no object then let's talk park frontage."

"Central Park?"

Her laugh was immediate. "Don't be ridiculous. They don't make blank checks with enough space for all those zeroes. A more modest park will be just fine."

"That's what you'd like? A mid-sized place with a heap of facilities facing a park in a nice neighborhood?"

She sat up carefully, wondering how she could cut out the chit-chat and get back to the physical intimacy. Their best-before clock was ticking. She rolled fully over and met his eyes. "Yes, Nathan. That is my fantasy apartment."

And fantasy it would remain because not only did she have extremely limited income but, out here in the real world, moving was not even on her radar. She was more than happy where she was. Comfortably settled.

Entrenched.

In fact, the thought of shifting away from all the people she'd filled her life with, and her apartment with its soft colors and mismatched furnishings made her stomach positively lurch. "Where is all this going?"

"I'm just—" his expression grew cautious "—getting to know you better."

She shifted to her side and tucked the covers in more firmly around her. "Why? You'll be gone in a few days."

Somehow, through all the thick shields she usually kept

around her heart, she knew that his next words would really matter. Her heart set up an insistent thumping.

A scowl marred those beautiful eyes and he looked as though he was on the verge of saying something difficult. But then the moment passed, and he shifted more comfortably in the bed and when he lifted his face again his eyes glittered with speculation. "Got something other than conversation in mind for the few hours until breakfast?"

If she hadn't spent the past five years keeping her own secrets she wouldn't have so easily spotted his. But there it was, laid out on the bed in front of them, metaphorically shrouded so that she couldn't quite make out its shape. Not that she had any real desire to find out. Look what had happened last time he'd shared something with her. And she only had one secret left to trade him….

"We could sleep," she said lightly, knowing full-well that wasn't an option. If they only had one night she wasn't wasting a second of it on oblivion.

He gave her that smile again. The one that turned her insides to mush. The one that made her forget anything but him. "Is that what you'd like to do?" he murmured as he stirred against her.

She stretched out along his length. "Nope."

"What would you like to do?"

Be yours forever.

The force of her mind's whisper slammed the breath clean out of her and robbed her of speech. They didn't have forever. They had until morning. Until the launch party…max. She knew that.

She *knew* that.

Why was her subconscious taunting her with thoughts of forever—with what she hadn't earned? Was it still playing cruel games? Or, worse, had she done the unthinkable and fallen harder than she realized?

"Tori?" He sat up more fully as she sagged back against the pillows. "Are you okay?"

Her heart pounded. "I'm…um…" What could she say?

I think I love you, Nathan.

Surprise!

Instead, she did what she'd been doing so well for the past five years: she pushed the emotion deep down inside and slid the I'm-okay mask firmly into place. "I just realized we don't have any more protection."

Nathan's gaze instantly heated up and he lowered his smiling lips closer to hers, which seemed to tremble and swell in anticipation. "Well, then we'll just have to get creative." She wriggled down lower in the bed and willed a smile to her waiting lips. He swiped his mouth back and forth across hers and his hand slid resolutely down to hook under her knee. "Lucky you're athletic."

It took only a cluster of rapid heartbeats for his talented lips and hands to gather her fully back into his command, to finely tune her body back with his. Tori's chest made the transition from tight pain to lancing desire immediately, her tattoo-heart switching rhythm easily. It was far too possible to let herself sink into the swell of rising passion rather than face the reality of what her subconscious had just tossed up.

Love.

The one thing she absolutely, categorically could not have with him. Or anyone.

Love was something you earned.

CHAPTER TEN

"TAKE it easy, Tori, they'll come."

She knew by Nathan's narrowed gaze that she was completely failing to mask her nerves as she wiped down the coffee and dining tables for the third time. It would have been the tenth if not for his solid, reassuring presence that grounded her. As much as was possible.

It didn't matter that she knew everyone invited to the webcam launch tonight. It didn't matter that she liked everyone invited. This was the first time she'd brought her neighbors together in one place in the entire time she'd been resident in this building, and she was insanely, inexplicably nervous. She wasn't stressing that her guests weren't coming…

She was stressing that they *were*.

Ironic. The high school senior voted Medford's most likely to have a beer with a President, and she was nervous about serving her neighbors a bunch of finger food.

She balled the sponge into her tight fist and returned it to the immaculate kitchen, then mentally reviewed everything that was laid out on the counter. Again. Not surprisingly, it was all exactly the same as the last time she'd counted it.

"Tori…" Warm arms slipped around her and drew her into rock-solid strength, gently halting her frantic cleaning. "It's going to be fine. Everything looks great and we've catered for a football team."

We've…plural.

Double tension scored her subconscious. It was bad enough having a party—she had no one but herself to blame for that—but the end of the party technically signaled the end of something else. There was no good reason for Nathan to return after the last party guest walked through of her shiny new door. The gathering had bought her a few extra days—of the most blinding, pleasurable intimacy imaginable—but nothing more. Nothing else had changed.

There had been no talk of anything more. Despite Nathan's occasional slips into plural.

She had enough self-awareness to realise that the falcons weren't the whole reason she was throwing this ridiculous party. She wanted Nathan to meet her neighbors. To get to know them. She wanted them to get to know him, to like him. This motley group of New Yorkers was her de facto family and, on some deeply buried level, she wanted their approval.

Even though it was completely and utterly pointless.

"I don't know why I'm so nervous," she said, snuggling in more tightly against his strength and pressing her cheek over his heart so she could hear its reassuring beat.

He gathered her in and touched quiet lips to her hair. Was he counting down the kisses to their last one the way she was? The way she had been since their first one? "You're launching a webcam. It's a big deal."

She tipped her head back to look at him—her favorite angle, up along that tanned, rough throat and jaw—and frowned. "No it's not. These are my neighbors. This should be nothing."

His eyes clouded. "Is it because I'm here?"

"I don't think so. I want them to meet you."

His lips tightened. "You do?"

"Well… You know. Without you there would be no webcam project."

She wasn't fooling him any more than she fooled herself. Not only was she apparently too chicken to have her neighbors over for snacks, but she was too afraid to let him see how she felt about him.

Coward.

Then again, courage was something she'd said farewell to five years ago.

Behind them a sharp rap heralded the exact moment the clock switched over to six o'clock. Trust someone to be uber-prompt. She stiffened her back, pulled away from Nathan and turned for the door.

Game on.

Angel the actress was unfashionably on time, standing in the hall with a bottle in her hand and a curious smile on her face, but others weren't far behind. Tracey and Neville Radcliffe, then Mr. Broswolowski, the deCostas. Her neighbors from either side. Tony Diamond from the end of the hall—the only real magician she'd ever known—turned up a bit late, but he'd taken the time to escort Nancy Smith down from her top-floor apartment.

They and a handful of other neighbors were mingling fabulously and exclaiming how odd that they'd not had more parties like this—the high-rise equivalent of a street party—while Tori faked endless tasks in the kitchen as her heart hammered and her mouth ran clean out of saliva. It wasn't quite as awful as she'd worked herself up to believe, but it wasn't entirely comfortable either. Very crowded. Very oxygen-depleted. Even with the safety windows slid open. More than ever, she longed for the vast, open spaces and arctic winds of the high mountain ranges.

She closed her eyes and tried to remember what that had felt like buffeting against her skin.

"Tori?"

Nathan swung past her servery for the seventh time, bending to see under the overhead cupboards and snaring her gaze. He'd been his typical charming self, winning over her neighbors, circulating, working the room. Tori envied him the apparent ease with which he could speak with interest to anyone about anything and have them eating out of his hand. Angel Santos was just about ready to have his children and she didn't even know he was rich as sin.

Tori had told them he was a friend and they'd been working on a project together, but that was it. It was Nathan's call whether he wanted to out himself as their landlord. Or her lover. So far he'd chosen neither.

Though glancing at him across the room, seeing his smile and secretly knowing what that mouth had done for her just hours earlier was the only thing that effectively distracted her from her annoying anxiety. And judging by the twist of his lips, he remembered too.

Were all sexually active people this smug?

"Everyone's getting restless," he said now. "Could be time for the falcons?"

"Really? Now?" As excited as she was to be launching the website, the idea of standing in front of people and speaking formally suddenly brought a hint of bile to her mouth. She frowned, remembering how many presentations she'd done to climbing groups back in Oregon. How effortless they'd been. Talking about things she was passionate about had never been an issue. "Can't you chat to them a bit longer?"

Nathan's brows dropped. "These are *your* friends, Tori. I'm doing my best—" and it wasn't until that moment that she realized how strained he actually looked "—but it's not me they came to see."

He moved around into the kitchen, positioned himself against the counter in such a way that his body shielded her from the view of her guests as he said gently. "You've climbed mountains, Tori. Talking about these birds should be nothing."

Should be. "Then why isn't it?" Her pulse chattered rapidly.

She was hiding in her own kitchen. She'd left Nathan holding the bag for entertaining her friends. She would have happily crawled back into bed right now until every last one of them left.

Oh, that was not good.

Her head came up. She glanced at the people milling around her tiny living room. She tuned in to the hammering of her heart. Then she looked at Nathan—his handsome face filled with patience and rather a lot of confusion.

She could do this.

She sucked in a deep breath, lowered the bowl she'd been filling with yet more unnecessary snacks and turned to her living room.

"Okay. Let's start."

And if he noticed *her* unintentional plural, he didn't say a word.

The room came buzzing alive as Tori spoke to them about the peregrine webcam project and how, despite other parts of Manhattan having them, theirs would be Morningside's first wildlife webcam. Her use of *theirs* had to be intentional and Nate watched her enthusiasm wash over every one of her guests like a seductive wave, despite her stumbling nerves at the start. In return, their growing excitement cross-infected her and she grew louder and more confident as she got closer to the moment of switching on the webcam monitor.

Her eyes glittered, her smile beamed. This was more the Tori he'd expected tonight. This was the Tori he'd selfishly lost himself in the past few nights. Radiant, courageous, wild Tori.

Timid kitchen Tori was not a side of her he'd ever expected to see. It threw him, though he knew how much she liked to work within her comfort zone. It just reinforced how little he really knew about her. How not-real this whole *thing* between them was. And it really shouldn't matter because in a few hours their *thing* would be over. The project was finished.

Neither of them had spoken of more.

Coming here tonight had been a risk. His heart had been in his throat since that first knock on the door. Wondering if he'd be recognized. Wondering if he'd bump into someone he used to see taking out the trash a lifetime ago. Could he rely on the vast physical changes between seventeen-year-old Nate and the man he was now? Getting into discussions about the bad old days was really not his idea of a good time.

But as more guests arrived and minutes turned into hours and no one said a word or even looked askance at him—beyond the obvious speculation in most expressions as to what his relationship with Tori was really all about—he'd realized that no one *did* remember him. And the only one he recognized for certain was Miss Smith, who remembered nothing at all most of the time.

"Here they are, Wilma and Fred." Tori activated the plasma with a theatrical flourish and every person in the room craned forward to see it. The screen glowed to life and caught Wilma in the middle of her regular bath, that talon-like beak rifling through slick brown feathers, completely unaware that she was being watched. Thirty days on eggs. Thirty days barely leaving that ramshackle nest.

That took a special kind of bird.

Or person. The thought flitted across his mind that Tori would have that kind of focus. Especially if it involved thirty days indoors. She did love her apartment.

He frowned. She really did.

She pulled up the website on the monitor and talked everyone through the various parts of it, showing them her photography, the live webcam box, the species information. The links to New York's other urban raptor sites.

Marco deCosta was the first to jump on the computer mouse and start effortlessly navigating his way around the detailed site—it was a healthy reminder that the sorts of tools Sanmore had grown great on were just commonplace for kids now. Marco's parents followed and then, one by one, everyone else began to explore.

Tori chatted to Tracey and Neville Radcliffe—the owners of that mad mini-horse, Gretel—and her origami-laundry friend, the theatre producer. She showed them through her photo album of raptor images. They hung on her words as though they'd never seen or heard about Tori's background at all.

Maybe they hadn't. The way he'd had to pry it from her determined lips…

Yet her neighbors had become so fundamental to her life here in Morningside. Like a regular mini ecosystem with every person depending on every other for some aspect of day-to-day life. Most aspects, in Tori's case. She'd be lost without her portfolio of trades. Life would certainly cost her a whole lot more.

And, once again, his chest tightened at the very real necessity of moving everyone out of the building. Of splitting up friendships. Of displacing Tori.

He'd opened his mouth any number of times over the past few days to tell her what he had planned. But every time he'd even looked as though he might be working up to some serious conversation, Tori cut him off, distracted him with a question, an activity, a kiss. Almost as if she didn't want to get deep and meaningful with him.

At least not emotionally.

The more time he spent with her the more he realized how much structure her days had. Not that his corporate days had any less, and not that she wasn't willing to throw it all to the wind in order to spend hours with him under the sheets. It was just…rigid—compared to how he imagined her earlier years must have been as a nature-loving, mountaineering tomboy.

But then she'd lost her brother and had stopped doing all the things she loved. Maybe it had changed her. Which didn't mean she wasn't capable of changing back. She just needed the right incentive. And less structure.

He maneuvered himself through the throng and closer to her side and took a risk—did something unexpected. Scandalously unscheduled. He slid his hand around her waist and onto her hip and whispered in her ear, "Anything you need from me?"

Her startled look back over her shoulder pleased him and worried him in the same moment. He loved that he could get her pupils flaring like that just with a touch, but the immediate way she stepped clear of his hold—smiling beautifully the whole time so nothing looked amiss to her speculative neighbors—and firmly put him at a distance…she did it all too naturally and he noticed it way too much.

…for a guy who didn't plan on being here past morning.

His stomach rolled. It was Friday. His time with Tori was up.

Tick-tock, tick-tock…

That bothered him a heck of a lot more than it should. The last thing he wanted to do on their last night together was spend it talking business. Talking about the demolition. He'd tell her personally, but not here.

Not tonight.

It took another hour to get the last of them out the door. The magician had left early to head off to a gig somewhere, forgetting that he'd escorted Nancy down. That meant she was the last person left sitting on Tori's sofa, an embroidered cushion clutched in her parchment hands.

"I'm missing *Ellen*," she whispered as Nate sank down next to her.

She'd been a ferocious television addict when he was a boy. Watching seventies reruns on the box while he did his homework at her dining table. Not interfering, not parenting, just being a friend. He slid his hand over her bird-like one and years of gratitude leached through that one touch. And he remembered that, for all his childhood challenges, there was light too. And lemonade.

"The party's over, Miss Smith," he said softly. "Would you like to go home now?"

He glanced over his shoulder, saw that Tori was busy saying farewells to Mr. Broswolowski at the door and turned quickly back to Nancy. "It's not much of a thank-you for everything you did for me, I realise." Having this conversation was no risk. It was like speaking into a vacuum. "But I've chosen your new home carefully." And though she didn't yet know it, he'd committed to paying her way until the end.

That was something he could do for her. To approximate how much she'd done for him.

"Everything rolls to its appointed end."

He stared at her. That was what her muddled mind chose to hold onto—*William Bryant?*

"I still have that volume," she said, quietly, and her eyes lifted to his. Decisively. His pulse thundered and his breath sucked out of his lungs. Her lips split into a gentle smile. "You always did enjoy it particularly."

Every bit of saliva decamped from his mouth. "You remember me?"

She turned those vacant eyes on him and they did seem a little less…absent. "It takes me a bit more time these days…" She squeezed his hand. "But yes. Welcome home, Nathan."

Blood rushed in torrents past his ears, almost drowning her out.

"I'm pleased you did so well in life," she said. "I so wanted that for you."

His throat tightened, which didn't make swallowing what little moisture he'd managed to generate any easier. He practically croaked his response. "Thank you, Miss Smith. For everything."

She looked back down at the cushion in her hands, lifted her face again and looked around. "Whose house is this?"

What? "This is Tori's apartment."

"Tori?"

A sinking feeling hit him. "You came to her party."

Her smile was beatific. "I love parties." And then she started to hum an old waltz tune, smiling to herself. Lost in memory.

Lost—again—to him.

He slid his other hand over hers and blinked back emotion. He'd never let himself ask as a boy. A point of pride. But he could ask it now. "Miss Smith, may I come up?"

She turned her radiant, vacant, aged face up to his. "Oh, yes!"

It took him an age to get her up two flights of stairs and settled back into her own apartment. She barely even seemed to know she'd been out. But she knew her household routines and she slipped straight back into them in a way that made him feel more comfortable about leaving her alone. She made a cup of tea, swapped her good shoes for slippers, turned on *Ellen* and promptly began watching as though he'd ceased to exist.

She had as much daily structure as Tori and had obviously grown extra reliant on it. Clearly, in her own environment, she was infinitely more in control of her faculties.

And he was about to tear her out of that. Guilt nagged, despite all the nursing care he'd bought her for the rest of her waking days. And, inexplicably, his mind went straight back to Tori. To the other woman who loved things just the way they were.

Even when she didn't.

He took the stairs in pairs in his haste to get back to her. It was going to be tough for him to come up with any decent reason to keep seeing her now that the webcam and the launch party were over. They both knew this was temporary, they'd both enjoyed it enough to stretch it out all week. Whatever move he made now was either going to send the wrong message, or bring an end to their short relationship.

Neither of which he wanted.

What he wanted to do was send the *right* message and have her give him the *right* answer.

Stay.

But he wouldn't. He might have failed—abysmally—in his attempts not to let himself care for her, but the one thing he did have from growing up almost completely responsible for himself was killer self-discipline. He'd give her a final night she'd never forget, tell her about the redevelopment and the new place he'd found her, make sure she knew what an amazing woman she was and then kiss her one last time.

Before leaving her apartment forever, honoring the commitment he'd made himself.

Viktoria Morfitt could do so much better than a workaholic with a shame-filled past and no interest in committing. But she wasn't going to find better while he was around taking up space.

"So the place survived the onslaught?" He made light as he came back through the door into the now-spotless apartment, critically aware that they only had a few more hours together. Though, as Tori turned to him with a blazing smile and moved with her catlike grace across the room, his whole body rebelled at the very thought. How could he be a man of steel resolve one moment and have it melt to a molten metal puddle the moment she locked him in her focus?

Just one more reason to get out now. While he still could.

"Nathan, thank you for all your help. I seriously don't think I could have got through without you."

"Sure you could. At worst you would have had to cut up your own carrot sticks."

She stopped before him, below him, and peered up through those enormous gray eyes. His heart started thumping.

"Let me be grateful, Nathan. You did help me." A shadow flitted across her face and was gone. "In ways I wasn't expecting. I don't understand why I was so nervous."

The heart-thumps turned into painful squeezes and he dug around for a way to keep things from getting any heavier. Ironic, given it had been her keeping things comfortably undemanding for the past few days, but if she asked him to stay forever right now he'd have a hard time saying no. Not that he thought for a moment she actually would ask.

His hands slid up her arms and around under her shoulder blades. "You want to show gratitude?"

A deep light flared in her gray depths. "Another massage?"

"No. No massage." At least not just yet. "But we will need to be lying down for it. If you're that grateful…"

She smiled and stretched her arms up around his neck. “Extremely grateful…”

And then her lips were on his and he forgot everything but the feel and taste of her.

CHAPTER ELEVEN

TORI woke to the sound of someone rummaging around in the kitchen—singing—and her sleep-addled mind immediately lurched into tightness. Into the past.

Rick!

But a bare moment afterwards, reality intruded as it did every morning and she remembered. Not Rick. Not anymore. But instead of the deep sorrow she had grown accustomed to carrying around for the first minutes of every day, a warm gooey honey washed over her instead.

Nathan.

That was his terrible singing coming from the kitchen. She lay back against the pillow and let the sadness leach away under the fresh breeze of her smile. There was something supremely endearing about a man who couldn't sing but didn't care who knew it. Nathan had the casual confidence only fortune and success could bring and, clearly, he had no need or value for perfect pitch.

Which was really just as well. She'd have to tell Pavarotti to tone it down before he scared Wilma right off her nest.

She pulled the sheet up under her arms and trailed it behind her out of bed and into the kitchen. She stood silently behind him and watched the way his powerful body moved through her kitchen. Decisively. With confidence. And he was only making breakfast.

No wonder he made love with such proficiency.

"It's Saturday, why are you dressed for work?"

Inane, yes, but even after three days she still wasn't used to morning-after conversation. In fact, she was thoroughly out of practice with conversation at any time of the day if you didn't count Gretel. And after what they'd shared last night, he was lucky she could even form sentences.

Nathan had made love to her as though she was made of blown glass. Slow, tender, beautiful. Long into the night. In a way that made it so hard to remember he was leaving.

But she suspected, because of that.

He spun around to face her and patted his coat pocket, the bulging one. "A CEO's diary does not discriminate."

He moved towards her, slid one hand behind her head and dragged his lips back and forth across hers, sending her pulse into riots and shooting spurs of desire straight to her core. If she'd expected regret she wasn't going to get any. He looked pretty darned pleased with himself. And painfully gorgeous.

"There's that smug expression I was telling you about," she said, sagging slightly against her pantry door.

The smile twisted into a full-blown grin. "Sorry, can't help it. You draped in a sheet standing in the kitchen like some kind of Greek goddess is going to take a little getting used to."

Going to? Those weren't the words of man who was packing his bags. The part of her that knew better did a little happy dance and it just felt so foreign. She stepped closer and pulled his phone out of his coat pocket and slid it behind her back. "So...does this mean you can hang around for a few more hours before yielding to your non-discriminatory diary?"

Lord, she didn't want him to go just yet.

He pulled her into the circle of his arms. "Do you want me to?"

She weighed her words. No point in denying everything she'd said and done last night. But old fears died hard... "I don't want you *not* to."

His eyes darkened and flicked over the place between her

breasts where one hand clutched the sheet to her. Then they lifted back to hers. "I have a couple of things I need to do."

"Is one of them kissing me?"

His gaze was shadowed. "Several of them involve kissing you. But also some work stuff." His eyes flicked away and returned. Then he reached around behind her and liberated his phone. "I also want to talk to you about something."

Oh. Her stomach dropped as she saw the fleeting doom in his expression. *This was it.* She took a mini breath. "Okay…?"

"Do you want to get dressed?"

Her heart constricted. She stepped back from him and pulled the sheet tighter around her body. "Do I need to get dressed?"

"If you want me to concentrate, yes."

Either that was a monumental save, just as her demons were surging to the fore, or it was the truth. "Okay. I'll be right back."

He called behind her, "I'll have coffee ready."

He did. And honeyed toast. It was all disturbingly domestic and more than a little alarming. Either he was going to tell her their time together was officially over—a proposition she'd been in serious denial about this week—or…

Nope. She had no idea what else it could be. The demons did exuberant laps in her mind as her pulse rate picked up pace to match them.

"So, I've been thinking about something you said the night we were first together…"

Heat immediately climbed. God, she'd said so many things. And groaned some. And cried some. And whimpered some. Most of them embarrassing.

She cleared her throat. "About?"

"About how you value honesty."

The demons retreated to hover nearby just in case they were needed on short notice, and they made room for a breath, albeit a tight one. "Okay. How about you just spit it out?"

"Delicately put." His smile completely disarmed her, as

usual. He leaned forward. "Okay, here's the thing. I may have found you a new apartment."

She stared at him. Of the million things he might have said to her just then… "I don't want a new apartment."

"It has everything on your list. Space, park view, trees, built-in facilities, in a good area, closer to me, actually…"

What list? "Nathan, I don't need a new apartment. Why would you look for one?"

His eyes grew cautious. "I'm not a terrible landlord, Tori. There's a reason Sanmore hasn't spent more on this building."

"*Asset strategy*, you said." And she hoped her snort told him exactly what she thought about his strategy.

"Right. But there's more to it." He studied her closely. "What would you say if I told you I was planning renovations?"

She sat up straight in her chair. "Renovations! Fantastic. We're so overdue for some work."

"Extensive renovations."

Her bubble burst. She frowned. "How extensive?"

"Very."

A nasty, twisty bite took hold deep inside and her stomach curled up to protect itself. "'Very' as in days of inconvenience?"

His eyes were as blank as she'd ever seen them, in awful contrast to the fiery passion of last night. "'Very' as in weeks, possibly…longer."

From nowhere, a deep panic started to take hold. Breathlessness. Dry mouth. Fast heart. Exactly the sort of thing she'd had when she first started climbing. She curled her rapidly cooling fingers into her palms. "Why are you telling me specifically?"

"Because we… Because I don't want it to be between us. Going forward."

The anxiety stirred her anger though she didn't quite understand why she was feeling either. Wasn't he just being honest with her? "I was under the impression there would be no going forward?"

His face was cautious. "Is that what you want? To end things?"

"It's what we agreed."

"I didn't have all the facts then."

"What facts?"

"I had no idea who you were. What we'd be like together." He cleared his throat. "How you'd make me feel."

She stared at him, crystallizing ice racing along her veins. "And now you do, you're keen to bundle me up and throw me into an apartment closer to you so you can reduce the mileage on your booty calls, is that it?"

His head jerked. "It's not like that. You know it's not."

"Then explain it to me, Nathan."

"I respect you, Tori."

"And?"

"And this is your home. I thought you'd want to know first. So you can plan."

She swallowed but there was nothing in her mouth to swallow "So this is more FYI than community consultation?"

"Tori…"

Her heart pounded. "The renovations are a done deal?"

"More or less."

"What about everyone else, Nathan? There's thirty-five households in this building. Where will they go for weeks on end?"

"I'm going to find each of them alternative accommodations. And pay their rent."

Her nostrils flared. "A good financial deal, but what about their day-to-day lives?"

"I've had my best people working on this. Finding good matches. A place close to his brother for Mr. Browoslowski. A small loft in SoHo for Angel. One block back from Riverside for the Radcliffes—awesome Great Dane country…"

Tori watched his lips moving but struggled to take in his words. The blood was rushing past her ears way too fast.

"A three-bed right over the road from Marco's school for the deCostas, a wonderful place with 24/7 medical care for Nancy—"

"You're putting her in a home?"

"It's not a home, Tori. It's an independent aged-care apartment. With daily medical assistance."

"No, *this* is her home, Nathan. Here. Where she's lived her whole life." Panic rushed up into her stomach and bubbled there.

"She's not safe here, Tori. How much longer before she *has* to move anyway?"

She ignored his logic. "And the deCostas' apartment?"

"I thought the proximity to Marco's school made it perfect."

"And how do you know where Marco goes to school? How do you know where the Radcliffes like to walk Gretel? How do you know where Mr. B's crazy brother lives?"

"Tori..."

She pressed her lips together. "Were you mining me for information every time we were together?"

"No, I wasn't. But I remembered things you told me. You *wanted* me to get to know my tenants."

"Not so you could throw them out on the street!"

His eyes glittered dangerously. "Do you *know* how much I'm spending specifically so that I *don't* leave them high and dry?"

Her whole body physically shook. "Don't throw your money at me, Nathan Archer. Don't come in here and exploit my party and my friends the way you've exploited me."

He hissed his frustration. "I did *not* exploit you or your party. I *carried* your party while you went all Greta Garbo on us. I just listened to—"

She shoved away from the table and to her feet, and marched resolutely away from him into the room where they'd spent so many extraordinary, precious hours together, slamming the door shut on so much more than the conversation and hauling the pillow that had so recently cushioned his head across her chest. Confusion and anger and seething anxiety all raged within her and overwhelmed her senses. She'd worked so hard to numb herself internally over the past five years. To survive what had happened in her family.

Her stomach lurched. What had she imagined would happen if she opened the door to more sensation? To love. To desire.

To trust.

How her subconscious must be cackling. It would have seen exactly where this was going to end. She'd broken the golden rule—she'd let Nathan close and tried to have something for herself. Maybe she should count herself lucky it was only her heart this time.

Last time she broke a golden rule, someone she loved died.

The doorknob started to turn and Tori squared her shoulders and took a deep, shaky breath. Nathan's beautiful dark head peered around the door. It killed her that her wounded heart still gave a pathetic little lurch at seeing him.

"Can I come in?"

She shuddered full-body. The ache intensified into a sharp blade that slipped neatly through the muscles between her ribs and poised over her heart. Three weeks ago he'd kicked the door in, desperate to save a stranger. Or had he just been in the building anyway, measuring up for all these renovations?

She pressed her lips together. "Suit yourself. It's your apartment."

How easily it came back to her: the careless shrug, the vacant stare. She hadn't used them since the days following Rick's fall. Her soul had been collapsing in on itself then, too.

His shoulders sagged. "Tori…I didn't use you to get information on your neighbors."

"So you say."

"Are you seriously thinking that an officer of the court

colluded to place me here so that I could get a handful of not terribly interesting facts about the tenants in the building?"

Tori fought the frown birthed by that irritating bit of common sense. But she couldn't hide it completely.

"Right." Nathan stepped toward her, nodding. "So none of this was planned."

"Then you're just an opportunist?"

"Absolutely, I built my business on capitalizing on opportunity. But I wanted to do the right thing by everyone."

"The right thing would be finding a different way to do your renovations. Floor by floor. Without disrupting everyone."

A dark shadow crossed his face. "It's not that simple."

Panic started to well. "Why can't it be? Why do you have to throw everyone's lives into turmoil?"

My life.

"This is a good outcome for the tenants. Six months free rent will set them up with a deposit on a better place, or a foundation to keep renting the places we've found them if they want to stay. Or time to find somewhere new if they don't."

"Do you imagine Nancy will think about it that way?"

"I don't expect Nancy to think about this at all."

"She's eighty years old, Nathan. This building is a part of her. Just because she's drifting off doesn't mean she doesn't know her essential surroundings. Or the people around her. She runs her life by the strict order in her apartment, her routines and patterns." Her pulse rate started to skyrocket and tiny pricks of light exploded behind her eyes. "Have you even considered that? I know she's a stranger to you, but she's like family to us."

His nostrils flared. "Yes, I've considered that. I'm getting just a little bit tired of you assuming I'm this corporate ogre come to sack the village before torching it. Every one of you is on a lease, Tori, including Nancy. A lease with an end date. By your own choosing."

She didn't want to hear his logic. "Where's your loyalty to

some of the people who've been on those leases for decades—?" *To the woman whose body you were sharing.*

Frustration hissed from his lips. "I've rewarded their loyalty tenfold. I sourced Nancy's new place personally and picked the best medical care I could find."

Everything began to spin and Tori couldn't grab all of the thoughts and images fast enough to force them into some kind of sense. She shook her head. "Why?"

"Because I—". He pinched his lips shut and changed tack. "Because she has no one else."

"What about the falcons? How do you think they're going to manage raising their young with the sounds of jackhammers pounding relentlessly behind them?"

"Seventy days, you said. To hatch, fledge and be independent. I've scheduled work to begin in seventy-five, so they should have moved on by then."

Her pulse began to hammer and dark spots flashed briefly across her eyes. She rubbed them and realized how damp her hands were. *Seventy-five days.* She had to be out in ten weeks. Hardly any time at all.

"You think they'll just fly away and come back next year? It doesn't work that way."

"According to your own fact sheet it does. Over generations. I can design the new building to be falcon-friendly. We'll have to trust that they return eventually."

Everything started to close in.

"Eventually?"

"You told me they're unlikely to breed again until their offspring move out into their own breeding territory."

Him being right didn't help. And him having thought a lot of things through carefully only boiled her blood more. She waved her hand out the bedroom door in the direction of the high tech monitoring gear. Her chest squeezed so hard it nearly stole the breath she needed to accuse him. She forced the words out.

"You knew the whole time you were installing everything,

designing the website, that it would barely get a few weeks of use? What a monumental waste of everyone's time."

His jaw clenched visibly. "It wasn't a waste. Look what it has achieved. The webcam wouldn't have had anything to show outside breeding season anyway. Just an empty box."

"Why didn't you just tell me about the renovations? We could have waited until after they were finished."

Nathan stared at her long and hard. "Because they won't be finished for some time."

Everything in her prickled at his tone. "How long?"

His eyes grew flinty. "Two years."

Her world lurched and tipped violently. "*Two years?* What the hell kind of renovations are you planning?"

"I wanted to talk to you about this, explain personally…"

"We're talking now. So explain."

His chest rose and fell on a controlled breath. Tori totally held hers. "I'm constructing a whole new building on this site."

Her blood froze over, her word barely more than a whisper. "What?"

"I'm demolishing this old building and erecting something new in its place. Something larger. More contemporary."

The knife poised between her ribs shifted trajectory and neatly pierced her lungs. All the air escaped in a pained whoosh. The room began to spin slowly. "No…"

"It's too young to have heritage status and too old to be economically maintained…."

His lips were moving but his voice warped in and out of focus in ears that thundered with sudden panic. *Demolition…* Her home. Her sanctuary.

"You can't…"

"It's all arranged." He frowned as he noticed her white-knuckled grip on the quilt. "Tori, are you okay?"

"You can't, Nathan. You can't." Her voice echoed in her head like a bad amusement ride. High-pitched. Discordant. But there was nothing she could do to stop it. "I can't."

"I found you a beautiful place, surrounded by trees. Right on the park. Only a few blocks from me. It's yours for a year. Longer if you want it. And if you want to come back here when the new building's up I can sort that, too."

His words washed in and out of her ears making little impact on her brain. *Coming back would require leaving.* The world dropped out from beneath her like the worst of free-falls. Except, abseiling down a rock face had never made her feel like this. She struggled valiantly to disguise how difficult it was to breathe. "I can't leave here, Nathan."

"Just come and check it out with me. I know you'll make it as nice as you've made this apartment. It has everything you spoke of that night."

She fisted his shirt and pulled herself closer to him, the fear clawing. "You're not hearing me. *I cannot leave here*."

He stared at her, then looked around and then back at her with a deep, pained frown. "Tori, what's going on? It's just an apartment. It's not like you'll be homeless."

What *was* going on? Her whole body was reacting. Trembling. But she fought to hide it from him. He wouldn't understand how important this apartment was to her, how much she relied on routine to get her through each day since she'd lost Rick.

She barely understood it. Although she feared she was beginning to.

Nathan took a deep breath and watched her through narrowed eyes. "When was the last time you went outside?"

The ridiculous question distracted her. "With you. On the roof."

"I mean out on the street. When did you last go through the front door?"

She blinked. It was easy to recall those first days when she'd moved in, when everything was furnished, unpacked and in its place. Then there'd been a bunch of trips into the surrounding neighborhood to get her bearings. Then ever-decreasing errands the more she set up trades within the building for things she needed. She really scraped her memory…

Her heart thumped.

…and came up blank.

Her brows drew together. Suddenly she saw the past five years played back in fast forward. Every time she'd hedged. Every time she'd stalled. Every time she'd ordered in instead of dining out. Every single trade she'd offered the people in this building to ensure that the world came to her….

So that she didn't have to go out to it.

And it frightened the hell out of her. When had her entire life become a series of carefully controlled, deeply comforting routines? Her pulse started to beat at the fine skin containing it.

"I…" But she had no idea what to say next.

His eyes flooded with pity. "Have you tried to get help?"

Help? "For what?"

"Tori. You haven't been outside in…what…years?" He shifted closer to her. "You're agoraphobic."

Her laugh sounded brittle, even to her and her breath grew painfully tight. "Don't be ridiculous. I'm a mountain climber. How can I possibly fear open spaces? You've seen me on the roof. On the ledge. All that wide-open sky…"

Deny that, genius.

But he couldn't. "It's still not normal."

She pushed away, her breath still straining. "Normal? Are you really sure you're fit to preach about what's normal?"

His eyes narrowed dangerously. "Tori…"

But she was in pure survival mode and, just like last time, her body was making the calls on how best to get through this. She felt her lips curl up. "You've driven yourself into the ground trying to prove something to a mother who probably never even noticed. Did she even know how rich you were at the end there? Where you ended up?"

"Don't make this about me, Tori."

Every time he said her name it was like a warning. His tight tone said they were at DEFCON three.

And she ignored it completely.

"Why not? Isn't this exactly about you? Your desire to make more money? Your desire to prove yourself and beat your sucky childhood? To build something shiny and expensive? Did you get your revenge that way, Nathan, living the high life while she lived in squalor?"

"This has nothing to do with her."

"Oh, really? Did you buy your mother her own apartment with park views, then? Or do you save that sort of thing for the women you're sleeping with?"

He glared at her. "She always had a safe roof over her head, until the day she died. I bought out her lease. And then I bought the whole building."

What? She took three steadying breaths. "How many buildings do you own?"

His eyes glittered like dead sapphires. "Just the one."

And with those three little words everything came together. Apartment 8B. The notorious Domino. The way he'd subtly avoided meeting any of the building's old-timers. The way he was neglecting the building to rubble.

"*This* is the place where you were so unhappy?"

His silence was assent enough.

A deep nausea washed over her. "You bought the building you grew up in. And now you want to tear it down. Have you even been back into your family apartment since she died?

More silence.

She stared at him. "And that strikes you as normal, does it? Have *you* tried to get help?"

Throwing his words so brutally back at him only served to crank him up to DEFCON two. But his anger was underpinned by visible pain. "This is business."

"Oh, please! Anyone else would just move away and move on."

The way you did? her inner voice accused.

"Columbia is looking for new student housing in the area, Tori. I'll make a killing."

"Then why didn't you just sell out to them years ago?"

"I wish I had," he ground out. "Then I never would have had to—"

He cut himself off way too quickly to ignore and pressed his lips against whatever he'd been about to blurt. Hurt twisted in her chest. "Meet me?"

"I was going to say 'have this ridiculous conversation.'"

The ice in her veins solidified that little bit more. "You don't think it's significant that you've only bought one piece of real estate in your life and it's your childhood home? That you're demolishing it when you don't have to?"

"It's business, Tori. Risk is what I do. Sometimes I win, sometimes I lose, but my instincts are seldom wrong." His nostrils flared wildly. "And at least I'm out there, living my life amongst real people."

"And I'm living mine here," she said, her voice painfully tight. "Just differently to you."

Both their chests heaved. "It's not living, Tori. It's just existing."

Her throat ached from wanting to shout at him. And from the strain of not crying. "Huh. Funny, these past few days have felt pretty alive to me," she said thickly. She'd been gradually thawing out since the moment he'd first caught her up in his smoky gaze. His smile. His kisses.

He swore under his breath and grudgingly met her eyes. "They were. I haven't felt so…connected… Ever."

She was only a deep breath away from hysteria. "Me, too. Let's celebrate by popping a cork or ripping down a building."

His lips thinned. "Your sarcasm's not shoring it up any. It's only reinforcing that nothing good comes out of this building."

Tori stared at him. "So this *is* personal?"

His face took on a wild hue. "No. It's not. But I won't be sorry that the building and its misery are gone. A nice side benefit."

"Is that what I was this week?"

His face turned ashen. "No. You were not." He swallowed hard. "But even you have to admit your life here hasn't been a riot."

"Sorry to bust your theory but my life was perfectly crap before I moved in here, thank you very much."

His face shuttered over. "Your brother."

She pushed to her feet, past him out into the living room. "Einstein."

He pursued her out the door. "You're here because of him."

"I'm here because New York offered me a new life. A fresh start."

"No." The intent look in his eye was too all-seeing. "You're living in the most crowded and anonymous city in the country on the money Rick left you, sequestered in this tower like some kind of twisted fairy-tale princess, banished from the people and mountains you love, punishing yourself."

She spun on him, clutching the pillow close to her chest. "Punishing myself—for what?"

"For living. When he didn't."

Every molecule of oxygen sucked out of her body, rearranged itself in the atmosphere and then flooded back in on a rush of heat. She marched straight up to him and every step was on razor wire. Fear gripped her deep and low. "You have no idea what you're talking about."

He towered over her. "Really? Do you imagine I don't know a thing or two about guilt? I was the unplanned pregnancy that cramped my mother's style her whole life. I was the irritating expense as I outgrew uniform after uniform at school. I was the reason she had to drop a days worth of clients to clean the fetid apartment once in a while for Social Services to come around." He stabbed stiff fingers into his chest. "I grew up thinking my mother sold her body to anyone who had need of it so that *I* could eat a warm meal each day. And to top it all off I had to deal with the guilt of being so damned *relieved* when I finally realized she was doing it for money and not for me."

Tori flinched at the pain in his face and her whole body cried out in sympathy.

"So yes, Tori, I recognise survivor guilt when I see it because I survived my childhood and it took me a long time to let myself be proud of that." He stepped closer. "You lived when your brother died. And you think that deserves punishment. But you're wrong. Living is a gift, Tori, and finding the right person to live that life with is more extraordinary than anything."

Tears surged suddenly from nowhere and spilled uncontrolled onto her raging-hot cheeks. Nathan's lips squeezed tight against saying anything more and he stepped toward her.

She stumbled back—desperate not to hear the promise in his words, desperate not to tempt the hand of fate by embracing the tantalizing hint of happiness he offered—and consciously euthanized everything they had built between them.

"I killed my brother, Nathan." Her voice was hoarse and unnatural. "I killed Rick to save myself."

The only sound in the entire apartment was the tight wheeze of her own tortured throat. Nathan didn't even breathe. He just stared at her in horror.

Totally deserved.

Tori swiped at the tears spilling down her cheeks. "He was so much bigger than me, hanging over that abyss. His weight was dragging us both over. It took forever, slipping closer to the precipice. I scrabbled and clawed and tried to arrest my slide but I couldn't get purchase. Rick couldn't climb back up and I couldn't hold him forever." She heaved in a tight breath. "We both knew what had to happen, but his left hand was twisted up in the rigging—he couldn't reach his knife."

Her eyes dropped to shake the image burned into her retinas. "He was screaming at me to do it before he dragged me over, but I couldn't. I wanted to save him or die trying. Because I loved him more than the air we breathed." A shudder racked her body and the tears stopped flowing. They sucked back into her stinging orbits. A numb stillness settled over her instead. "But I got within a meter of the edge and, in that moment, right at the last moment I realized I was too afraid to fall. To die. So I did it. I held my breath, released my knife and cut the rope. And he fell."

Endless silence followed. And why not—there was nothing more to say. She'd said it all five years ago to the relentless line of strangers who investigated the accident. Nathan stepped towards her and she stepped back, crossing her arms in front of her.

His voice cracked when he finally spoke. "You had no choice. You would have both died."

She lifted anguished eyes to his. "I wish I had. Everything I've done since is just taking up air."

"No..."

"Maybe I am punishing myself. But Rick will never laugh or cry or be loved or watch sunsets or hold a sleeping child in his arms. Why should I get to?"

"So...what—you're just going to rot here in this apartment? Forsaking any goodness that might creep in under your defenses? Until you're old and senile and die alone in this apartment?"

Her chest squeezed hard and she thought immediately of Nancy. Was that why she felt so close to the older woman? Because she saw herself in Nancy? She straightened her back and the effort half killed her. Nathan was handing her the perfect excuse to end things between them. To do what she knew she had to. It would be better for him in the long term if she just unraveled the complicated tangle that had formed from her heart to his and tore it away.

She closed her eyes. In her mind she lifted a knife to the rigging of whatever it was that had brought she and Nathan together. Held them together now. "Yes." She took a long breath. "Starting with you."

He stared at her, his burning regard dark in bleached skin. But something about the raw pain she saw swilling in the twin depths made her pause her mind's knife. Offer him—

them both—one last chance. "Will you leave the building standing?"

His nostrils flared and his eyes blazed at her. "I can't, Tori. Not just because you can't go outside..."

Air sucked into her lungs of its own accord and it was strangely reinforcing. But it didn't do a thing to diminish the ache that filled her.

He wouldn't do it for her.

Because his own reasons were too strong.

Her heart cracked wider. "Then I don't want your new apartment. Or your charity."

She crossed to the refridgerator, snatched free the single sheet of paper stuck to its front and scribbled across it with her pen. His community order, fully signed off. She pushed it into his chest, and sliced the knife clean through the final golden filaments binding them together.

"And I don't want you to come near me ever again."

The ghosts of the building held their breaths.

Nathan stared at the order and then at her, deep and unreadable, although his chest pumped hard. "This is not really about the building, Tori." But then his lashes dropped and he twisted away and flicked a business card out onto the counter. "When you decide you need help—when you decide you need me—you know where I am."

She held herself perfectly rigid as he moved toward her front door. The door that had somehow come to symbolize her: as hollow and out of place as she always felt.

Except when she was with Nathan.

He stopped at the door and looked back at her, burning to say something. But he glanced down at the floor and then lifted carefully blank eyes back up to her and murmured a few words before disappearing out the door.

Tori waited until she heard the door latch quietly closed and then she took the pillow still smelling of him and hurled it, internalizing her scream so that it hurt more. So that the memory would be branded into her soul. So that she'd never again forget why she didn't let anyone in. Why she'd embraced this careful, controlled world where everything happened in the same way every time.

She and Nathan were not meant to be together. It was hard enough finding a perfect match for your outward qualities without also expecting your raging demons to get along. There was more than one way to be incompatible.

It had been a long time since her body had harbored intense pain—her routines and rules and cloistered ways had done their job in holding it at bay—but she felt it now, surging back in, raw and razored, at the thought of losing the man she'd only just found.

The man she hadn't even known she needed.

Her heart squeezed into a twisted pulp.

She stared around her now at the familiar sanctuary of her apartment. Her old furniture. Her familiar view. Her entire world. And she knew that, even if it *had* tiptoed up on her and taken over her life, this apartment was directly responsible for keeping her alive these past five years. For helping her breathe. For letting her heart beat. And it was going to be ripped into tiny pieces and hurled to the pavement at the hands of a man she'd given herself to, body and soul.

Nathan was going to rip her out of her safe life the way he'd come into it. In an explosion of timber shards.

*Forgive yourself...*he'd said right before he disappeared through her open doorway. But then he'd whispered the rest, and she'd almost not heard him over the roar of her frantic heartbeat past her eardrums. *Forgive yourself for choosing life that day...*

She folded her arms over her head and sank down onto the floor, releasing the pain on a stream of hot, blinding tears.

...but not for wasting it.

CHAPTER TWELVE

"You'd better get up here, Nathan. There's a woman hanging from your building and there are an awful lot of people starting to gather."

The moment Nate retrieved Dean's voice-mail message he knew exactly who the woman was and what she had done. He slid over to his desktop and fired up Sanmore's latest internet browser. He hadn't visited the webcam in a couple of weeks—every time he did it only reminded him of Tori's warm little apartment, of the wild, beautiful birds, and the wild, beautiful woman who cared for them. It reminded him of what he no longer had a right to dream of at night. But he still kept the link in his favorites folder. And he still hovered the mouse over it from time to time. The only thing that stopped him from clicking it was that he felt vaguely like a stalker.

She'd made it perfectly clear she wanted nothing more to do with him and he'd always been a man of sterling self-discipline. To the point of pain.

But better him in pain than her.

The website loaded and he paused for a nanosecond to look at some new imagery on the homepage—two robust, browning chicks that had been tiny balls of fluff the last time he'd checked.

His eyes flicked to the visitor-counter and widened, seeing a number in five figures. Low five figures, but still…That was a lot of people checking out Morningside's raptors in just a few weeks.

In the top corner, something about the thumbnail for the webcam didn't look right. As if it was blocked by something. He activated the cam and held his breath while it loaded.

"Oh, you are kidding me…"

There *was* something blocking the camera's view of Wilma and the chicks. A piece of card, propped up by a soda can, and kind of off center as though the wind—or an inquisitive falcon—had knocked it askew. It had a bold message in Tori's handwriting scrawled in thick, black ink.

Help save Morningside's falcons.
Help save their building.
Add your voice to the protest.
4:00 p.m., June 23

And that would be today. Nate's lashes drifted shut.

But then he couldn't help smiling. A normal person would have added a tastefully bordered HTML message to the homepage with five minutes' work. But Tori did nothing the normal way and her personalized message achieved two things. It added some raw urgency to her plea, which site fans would immediately respond to, and it blocked the birds from the view of those ten thousand plus visitors, effectively doing exactly what demolishing the building was going to do. Make them disappear. Which the site users wouldn't like. Maybe enough to get off their butts and travel up to Morningside for the protest that started—he looked at his watch—ten minutes ago.

Tori was an accidental genius.

And a total thorn in his side. She haunted him at night. She troubled him during the day. He caught himself making business decisions he thought she, rather than his shareholders, might approve of, and he spent way too long each day obsessing on which tenants had begun to move out and waiting to see her name show up on the report. So far most of the neighbors he knew had shifted to their new accommodations, even Mr. Broswolowski, whom he'd figured would have stuck in there with Tori. But he'd personally signed off on Mr B's relocation expense just two days ago so—other than Miss Smith who was scheduled for the end of next week—Tori was all out of friends in that big building.

Who was looking after her now?

The tenants' deadline was up in just a week. But if she was planning eleventh-hour protest rallies then she wasn't going anywhere soon. That meant she was holding out for the bailiffs. Or she was still in denial.

He groaned.

She didn't have a textbook phobia—that would be too simple and Tori was everything but simple. She had developed her own special blend of dysfunction; one that made her overly reliant on her ordered, predictable world, to counteract the damage she'd done by choosing life that day on the mountain. He'd looked into it to understand. To see if it truly was a big enough deal to throw away everything they'd shared. Apparently it was.

And accepting that was one of the hardest things he'd done. Forcing Tori back into the world would only hurt her more. Between them, they had two lifetimes of damage conspiring to keep them apart. And it wasn't often he met someone who trumped him in the screwy stakes.

He asked himself, again, what he'd been secretly asking himself for weeks—what she'd asked him.

Was she right? *Was* he demolishing Morningside for the wrong reasons? He had a written expression of interest from Columbia University's legal department telling him otherwise but he *could* have sold them the building right away. Let them do all the dirty-work with the tenants.

His heart heaved.

Let them throw Tori's world into disarray.

He missed her. Even the screwy parts. He missed the way she teased him mercilessly and laughed at him if he tried to talk up his achievements. He missed her warm body against his at night and the incredible rightness of being joined with her. He missed the wonders that he got to teach her and the amazing wilderness stories she got to teach him. He missed turning up on her doorstep at 4:00 p.m. sharp, knowing the day was just getting going.

But he didn't miss hurting her. Or forcing her to look at things she wasn't ready to face.

His gut lurched. He'd hated that.

He'd had a full private session with the psych that he'd lined up for Tori ready for the day she called him to ask for help—not that she ever would call, and the psych knew that even if it had taken Nate a while to catch on. He'd told Nate that forcing Tori back into the world was the fastest way to ensure she never healed. And given she'd thrown him out of her life for good, helping her more gently wasn't really an option. He could only hope that the looming eviction deadline would trigger some kind of change. But he'd expected it to be in the form of sticking an experimental toe out the front door.

Not arranging a rally for a thousand wildlife fanatics.

He could only imagine how intensely uncomfortable the very idea would have made her. Which said a lot about how desperate she must be feeling. And desperate people did desperate things. Like making a nestful of birds seem in more danger than they actually were.

Help save Morningside's Falcons.

Might as well have said *Please help me.*

He winced and snatched up his desk phone. "Karin, can you get the car out the front? I'm going uptown. And then get on to Tony d'Angelo at the NYFD…"

When he arrived, Simon had to let him out up the block because 126th Street was gridlocked thanks to the mix of people spilling out of the laneway behind his building. Young hippie types, older retired types, backpack-wearing corduroy types. Mothers with children. Hundreds of people. Traffic was still getting through, but it was car by car and walking pace to make sure no one got hurt. On foot was definitely faster.

Nate rounded the corner just as he had that first day and elbowed his way through the milling crowd, dodging the odd placard before it took his eye out. He glanced upward immediately.

And then his stomach flipped.

Dean wasn't kidding when he'd said *hanging from your building*. Tori dangled from the bedroom ledge one floor up from hers, fully rigged out in climbing gear, with a brightly decorated bedsheet saying Save Morningside's Falcons furled out below her. It took him only a blink to realize that she couldn't have opened 11B's bedroom window, so she must have climbed down the outside of the building to get to the ledge.

Crazy fool woman!

He looked around. The crowd was looking uncertain. Like a mob who'd forgotten why they were at a lynching. A bad feeling settled in his stomach.

"What's going on?" he asked a woman standing nearby. "Why isn't she doing anything?"

The woman shrugged. "Everyone was cheering as she shimmied down the building and unfurled the banner—" his stomach dropped clean away at that image "—but then she kind of just…stopped. We're waiting for something to happen."

"You care what happens to these birds?"

"Well, sure. There's not a lot of community spirit around these days. And *she* cares. Look at that. Who does that?"

His gaze followed the woman's finger upward again. There was definitely something spectacular and inspiring about a woman clinging like a backward starfish to the outside of a building. But then he narrowed his eyes and looked at Tori's posture.

Really looked.

She kind of just…stopped.

Nate sucked in a breath. Not stopped. *Froze.*

He sprinted for the building, fighting his way through more

and more people who were arriving and packing into the small space below until he got around to the fire exit at the base of the stairwell. He pulled his keys out and sorted through them until he found the one he needed and then flung the doors wide before running inside. The elevator would take a lifetime to get up there and Tori might not have that long. So he stuck to the stairs, not even counting the floors as his long legs ate them up.

By the fifth floor they protested and by six they shook with a hot burn. But the image of Tori hanging, terrified, from the building filled his mind and drove him onward. He visualized a scenario in which he got up there and she yelled at him for interfering. Called the cops on him. Slid her hands onto those beautiful hips and glared impatiently because she was actually *perfectly fine*, just…taking a breather.

He'd take that. He'd love that. Because it would mean she was okay. It would mean she was coping.

But deep down inside he knew she wasn't. She hadn't been coping for a really long time but she'd had everyone fooled. Her parents. Her neighbors. Him.

Herself.

Sometimes even the unrescuable needed rescuing.

As he passed the seventh-floor landing, his lungs pure agony, Nate realized that he wasn't going to be able to pull Tori up from the ledge outside 11B's sealed bedroom pane and there was no way he'd fit through her bathroom window. The only way he was getting her down *was* down and the only apartment that would put him close enough for that was his own.

His mother's.

His throat threatened to close right over and end it all here on the steps. He pushed through the landing doors and took a sharp left. The whole floor was ominously quiet, with most of the building now vacant. It practically echoed with the sound of his racing feet.

He didn't waste time searching for that little bronze key, hurling himself instead at the locked door. His whole left side screamed on impact but the door creaked and shuddered. He backed up and slammed again and the lock burst from its frame, throwing him hard into the middle of what his mother used to call the "receiving" room.

There was only one thing he'd received there and that was an awful, early education.

The apartment was musty with age and dank with mildew but otherwise empty of anything that would have identified it as his. He'd donated the entire contents to Goodwill when his mother had died and had called professional cleaners in to scrub any echoes of their life from the nicotine-stained walls. But memories still reached out and snatched at him as he pushed himself to his feet and ran through to the bathroom. The window resisted at first but he forced it open and stretched through it.

"Tori!"

He couldn't see her but he heard her tentative response, tight and small. "Nathan?"

Everything in him threatened to go wobbly at the sound of her fear. But he forced himself to stay strong until she was safe again.

"Tori, can you get back up?"

"I…I can't. I can't move…."

She sounded so much more than scared. Angry. Incredulous. Distressed. Heartbroken.

He craned his neck around to the left and saw an old lump of concrete sitting on the ledge. Dangerous, but maybe the only way. He took a deep breath. "Tori, I need you to turn completely away from the building. Can you do that? Face the Hudson."

He listened for her response but only heard a mewling sound that could have been "yes" or could have been the falcon chicks two storys up expressing their displeasure at the disturbances going on all around them. He slid back through the window, then wiggled an arm through ahead of him, just long enough to reach the concrete lump. He grabbed it and brought it back through into the bathroom. Then he sprinted through the old kitchen, stripping off his tie and shirt as he went, and wrapping them thickly around his right hand and forearm before fitting the stone back into his swaddled fist.

His hands shook so badly he nearly couldn't tie off the swaddling. *Tori...*

In the master bedroom he yanked back the old curtains and a decade of mildew and dust exploded into the air. Nate fixed his eyes on the view outside, determined not to visualize what this room had once looked like or what had gone on here. He saw Tori's shoulder down at ledge level and the head she'd screened with her arms to shield it.

He lifted the rock and slammed it against the edge of the glass farthest from her.

The window cracked on first impact and smashed outward on the second. Glass fragments went everywhere and he hoped he'd managed to control the spray so it fell on the ledge and not on the protesters below. Tori turned toward him, wide-eyed and pale.

And wildly, patently, relieved.

His determination doubled. He used his wrapped fist to punch out the entire left hand pane of the bedroom window and then sweep the worst of the glass into the corner of the ledge. Then he unraveled it and threw the shirt aside and boosted himself out the window before he thought too much about the danger of what he was about to do.

Or how high he was.

Eight storeys seemed to swim in and out of focus below him. One minute the people below were just a bright sea of color and the next he was making out the tiniest and most inconsequential details. An overly large nose. A Lakers cap. And all of them with one expression in common—wide-eyed, excited disbelief that *someone else* was now climbing out onto the building's exterior. A half-naked man.

So much better than video games!

Nate dragged his focus back to the woman he loved and tried not to think about how far away the hard ground was and what it might do if he was to suddenly rush toward it. Or if she was…

Because he did love her. And it took a ridiculous incident to make him acknowledge it. He'd been half in love with her when he'd first kissed her in that elevator. And then their week together as lovers had sealed the deal. He'd loved her then but not been able to admit it.

Any more than he was prepared to admit she was right about this building.

Because he feared he'd be as bad at love as his mother and as just blind to his own failings.

"Tori…"

"Nathan, be careful!" Her eyes were as wide as those of the people in the crowd below.

He slid down into sitting position and hung his legs over the edge, close to where she hung suspended and the world lurched sickeningly. "I could say the same thing. What are you doing?"

"I'm trying to save the building!"

Even speaking made his chest ache. Five kinds of fear congealed in his lungs. "By fixing yourself to the outside of it? You think you wouldn't just be a convenient target for the wrecking ball?"

Slipping straight back into their usual, bantering dynamic helped take his mind off the fact that his entire future hung suspended in space and so, practically, did he. Joking seemed to help Tori, too. She loosened up just a bit.

"I used 11B's bedroom ledge to come down from so I didn't disturb the birds. I just wanted to hang the banner but then I looked around. At all the people. And I just… Everything just…" Her face folded.

He reached forward with his legs and hooked them around the taut rigging that held her weight, and she lifted her arms and grabbed his ankles immediately.

His smile was half grimace. "You've done this before."

Her voice tightened through clenched teeth. "This isn't the first time I've gotten into a tricky spot while climbing."

He swore and didn't bother to disguise it. "I kid you not—when I get you in you are never leaving the house again."

The irony of that made them both laugh, tight and strained. Nate locked his abs, tilted back onto his coccyx and contracted his legs back toward his body. The first little bit wasn't a problem because the rigging offered no resistance, but as he pulled, even Tori's slight weight dragged him forward a bit and he had to grip the concrete with what little nails he had. She turned in his grasp until she was facing him. The deathly pale bleach of her skin sunk home.

He had a sudden and crystal-clear vision of her, tear-streaked, exhausted and scrabbling inexorably down a mountain face, trying desperately to hold onto her brother while her heart ripped apart. He knew how he would feel if he dropped her now.

His life would be over.

A deep and a biding purpose flooded through him. He was going to build her a new life. "Hold on, baby. I've got you."

She locked her eyes on his, pale and frantic. "If you slide, you let me go."

He pulled harder and grimaced past the pain. "Not going to happen."

Her breathing was fast and urgent. "I'm rigged, Nathan. You're not. If you start to go you just let me go. I cannot lose you."

Lose you.

Not "lose you *like this*".

Absurdly, given the peril that they both faced and despite the deathly drop below him, his heart lifted. "You belong in my arms, Tori. We're not stopping until you're back there." He wriggled into a surer position. Every part of him protested. "The longer you talk the weaker I'm getting. Now shut up and start climbing."

She was still too low for the ledge, but she wasn't too low to climb his legs. She gasped a few instructions on how he could best brace himself and then she twisted the rigging in her fist and used it to take the bulk of her weight while her other hand clasped hard around his thigh for purchase.

She pulled. He braced. Then he tightened his legs under her armpits so she could release the rigging and reach for a higher point. She did, hooking her free hand onto his belt. It was worth every one of the designer zeroes it had cost as it helped pull Tori up and half across his lap.

So close.

He let go of one of his brace points and wrapped his arm around her torso and then used every fiber in every thread of every muscle in his body to pull them both back into a prone position on the filthy, pigeon-poop-covered ledge.

It might as well have been a down comforter.

He circled his screaming arms around her and pulled her hard up against him, the rigging protesting at the stretch, shards of broken glass slicing into his unprotected back.

Tori scrabbled to release the clips that kept her from Nathan and when the tethers swung free there was a joyful cheer from the crowd below. She flung her arms around him, reveling in the feel of his hard, shirtless body against hers, and she twisted her legs sideways so that one hundred percent of both of them was supported by flat concrete ledge. No chance of him sliding off.

No chance that she'd kill another man that she loved.

She buried her face into the sweat-covered curve of Nathan's neck and inhaled the heated scent raging off him. Every part of her started to shake and he absorbed her tremors straight into his skin. It didn't matter that the last time she'd seen him she'd thrown him out of her apartment. Her life. That she'd confessed her greatest shame to him and he'd accused her of wasting the life she'd chosen that day on the mountain face. That he'd lied to her about where he'd grown up. And that he was going to destroy her home.

All that mattered was that Nathan was here. In her arms.

And his heart was beating sure and hard and eternal against hers. For whatever minutes they had together.

She'd take it.

Eventually he spoke, his voice cracked and gravelly against her ear. "Are you hurt?"

Only inside. From so much. She shook her head.

"I need you safely inside, Tori. Can you stand?"

Her eyes dropped to his biceps. "My muscles aren't the ones twitching with exhaustion. Can *you* stand?" His color hadn't come back yet.

"Don't worry about me," he said. "You first."

She scrabbled over him, knowing he wasn't moving until she did. And more than anything in this world she wanted carpet under his feet. And, for the first time ever, under her own. She practically tumbled into the empty apartment and then rolled away from the window to make room for Nathan.

Through the window that was so much like her own, she watched him pull himself into sitting position on the ledge and sucked in a pained breath as she saw the shards of bloody glass sticking out of his back like some kind of masochistic body art. She glanced around and saw his torn-off shirt on the floor. She had it ready when he finally slid through the shattered window and landed with a thump next to her on the floor.

He looked baffled by his own weakness.

"Fatigue," she croaked. "And shock. Give yourself a minute for the adrenaline hit to pass." But then she lunged toward him and snagged his shoulder just as he might have leaned back against the musty apartment wall. Against the forest of broken glass peppering his skin. "You're going to hurt any moment, too."

She saw the moment he did. As the pain of thirty slices registered on his handsome face. The face she'd believed she'd never see again.

Compassion washed through her. She crawled around behind him and sat, spread-eagled, with her thighs either side of his hips to keep him from slumping backward. Worrying about him kept her from thinking about herself. About what had just happened. Just like getting Rick help gave her something to focus on when he died.

To hold herself together.

"Hold still." She picked at the larger pieces of glass, wincing as Nathan flinched. The easing of the blood confirmed they weren't as deep as she'd feared.

His voice was strained and low as he said, "Don't ever do that to me again."

"I have to get the worst pieces out—"

"I'm talking about the stunt you just pulled. I'm talking about looking up from a crowd full of strangers and seeing you hanging there, petrified, and at risk of falling."

Petrified. She had been, too. Completely overcome with an emotion that just froze every living part of her. Until she'd heard his voice… Her body shuddered with remembered relief. She picked more glass out and softly stroked every spot where she hurt him before moving on to the next. Then she paused.

"I don't know why…" She frowned at the unmistakable breathlessness of anxiety rising in her chest. Climbing was all she'd had left of her old life. "Do I not even have that now? I can't even climb a building without freaking out?"

He reached his right arm around behind him and curled his hand around her hip, holding her tightly against him. "I don't care. I'm just glad you're okay."

The awkward, tender touch broke her in a hundred places and gave her the strength to whisper something she'd realized as soon as she turned out there on the building face and saw all those people below her. All that vast, unfamiliar city stretching out beyond her. What he'd been trying to say the last time they spoke.

When she'd said such awful things to him to distract her from the truth of his words.

"I'm not okay, Nathan." Her eyes stung from so much more than the summer glare coming in the window. Her body heaved with a sob bursting to express itself. "I haven't been okay for five years."

He twisted around to see her but the pain of his shrapnel back stopped him with a jerk. Instead, he brought his left arm up over those powerful shoulders and snaked it around her neck and pulled her hard against his damaged flesh as though he just didn't care. Tori pressed her face against the hard angle of his jaw and did her best not to injure him further.

They both needed the contact before all else.

"I was terrified I was going to fall," she whispered against his ear.

He pressed his face back into hers. "There are much worse things than falling."

God, how true that was.

He turned toward her, bringing his lips mere millimeters from hers. But it wasn't their lips that met, it was their gaze. His breath was warm and comforting so close to her as he spoke. "Fear is good, Tori. It's normal. It means you have something to lose. Not fearing means not caring."

She frowned. How long had it been since she stopped caring about life?

"I tried to come to you."

His eyes darted towards her. "When?"

"About two days after you left. I wanted to show you I could. Show myself. But I didn't get past the sidewalk." She pressed her lips together to stop them trembling. "That was when I knew it had gone far enough. Knowing how I felt about you and still I couldn't…."

Her eyes misted over and tears choked her. She rested her chin on his shoulder, glad she couldn't see his reaction to her inadvertent declaration. "What's happening to me, Nathan? I'm normally the master of my fear."

"You haven't been mastering fear, you've been minimizing it. Avoiding it, by controlling your environment so tightly."

Her heart protested with a violent lurch. She traced her fingers carefully across his back and resumed picking at the glass, the hypnotic actions clearing her clouded, cluttered mind and forcing her chest to ease. Nathan settled back against her fingers and let her do it, giving her the breathing space she needed.

Was that what she'd been doing—avoiding her fears rather than facing them? She'd told herself she wanted to be safe... But maybe it was more that she wanted to be *Safe*—uppercase. She'd built herself a complicated world that meant she never had to jeopardize her boundaries, meet strangers, risk loss. A world that had seemed complete and varied and even rich until she shoved it up against the world of someone like Nathan and realized how homogenized and...beige...hers had become.

Worse, browned with stale air.

"I don't want to be Nancy. I don't want to live a life without risk. Why would I do that to myself?"

He spoke again, soft and close. "Two people died on that mountain, Tori. Except one of you kept breathing."

Everything in the room stopped. Pulse. Noise. The tiny particles of dust that danced like fairies in the shafts of light streaming in the window. Was that what she'd done five years ago? Stopped living? Was she truly the walking dead? In a rush of awareness she realized that was exactly how she'd been feeling for...a long time. Despite the neighbor friends. Despite the keeping busy. Despite the secret dreams of "one day."

Until a knight in such thick shining armor had barged his way into her familiar apartment and her safe, ordered life all those weeks ago.

Her breath resumed and the dust-fairies fluttered downwards. She pulled the final glass shard from his shoulder blade, kissed the vacant spot it left and then left her lips pressed to his flesh and murmured, "I feel alive right now."

Anyone else would have heard it as a come-on. But not Nathan. Because they were too similar. He knew her heart was suddenly beating as hard and as enthusiastically and as *vitally* as his. He knew her fear was still pulsing through her system, waking every long-dormant cell in her body with the clanging of bells. He knew how her flesh sang when it came anywhere near his.

Because he was part of her, too.

"It's what we do to each other," he said. "We bring life."

She wiped away the final trickle of blood and tossed the last glass shard to the tiny pile a few feet away from them. Then she pressed herself fully against his back as if to stem the claret floodtide. She slid her hands around under his arms and flattened them against his hot steel chest and let his strength soak into her.

"How do you know me so well?" she whispered.

He took an age to answer. "Because I am you."

She sat up straighter and he twisted around, bringing her half around onto his lap. "What do you mean?"

"Look around us, Tori. Where are we?"

It was only then she stopped to wonder about the empty apartment they were in. There was no way that the fastidious Barney would have let his apartment get like this, even before moving out last week. Which meant they were two floors down and not one. Which meant this was—

She sucked in a breath. "Your mother's apartment."

"I haven't set foot in here in sixteen years."

She glanced around. "Looks like no one has."

Sealed up as tight as his wounded heart. Tori sucked back an ache. It would have been bad enough hearing the raw pain in his voice without also seeing it tarnish those compassionate, brilliant eyes. "And you never came back here? Except to buy the building?"

His lips pressed extra-thin. "Even then I did it through a proxy. I had no interest in setting foot in this place. Ever."

Tori's stomach squeezed for him. "You planned to demolish it even then?"

"No. At first just owning it was enough. It was a statement I thought I was making for other people. For her, maybe. But I think I was really convincing myself of something."

Tori slid her hand up to cup his cheek. "Of what?"

Two pained creases appeared between his brow. "That I'd made it. I'd survived."

She stroked him carefully. "Those memories are part of who you are."

"Not the best part."

She winced at the self-loathing in his expression. "No. But they forged the best part. You can't deny them any more than I can pretend Rick's death never happened."

Much as she'd been trying. No photos. No family. Avoiding.

Oh.

And just like that, the light streaming in the window might as well have shifted and fallen directly on them because the truth blazed golden and obvious down on the two of them, curled around each other on the filthy apartment floor.

They'd both enshrined their memories to protect themselves. She'd chosen to sequester herself away from hers. Nathan had entombed his whole childhood in this room.

"Were there no good times at all, Nathan?" Had he slid the stone shut on everything that happened?

Pain sliced across his face, more serious than the superficial wounds on his back. Those would heal. He looked around and shook his head. "It's hard to remember a single one. Not in here."

"Would you have felt differently about what she did for a living if she'd not been such a miserable parent?"

His eyes grew round with pain and then incredulity. "I just can't even conceive of her as a better mother."

She turned her hand and ran the backs of her fingers over his jaw. "What if she was disappointed in herself? That she wasn't a stronger person?"

"Then her whole life must have been a disappointment."

Tori frowned. "Imagine living with that. Knowing it was true." Nathan stared at her. She held his gaze. "I know something about self-loathing, Nathan. After a while it's hard to imagine you have any worth at all. It becomes possible to justify anything."

Look what she herself had justified.

His pain—old and entrenched—swamped her. "Hating her hurts you."

"I hate what she did."

Tori took a breath. "I think you hate what she didn't do."

"What's that?"

Gently, gently. "Put you first."

His eyes spat pain. "Isn't that what mothers are supposed to do?"

She thought of her own. The grieving woman she'd carefully partitioned out of her life rather than let comfort her. The woman who'd lost two children that day.

"Yes, it is. But when you're fighting for your psychological life there's not a lot of room for anyone else." Unless they force their way in. She curled her free hand around his as a silent thank you. "A lot of years can go by in the void, Nathan. It's a miserable, lonely place."

He stared at her, a deep frown cutting between blue, blue eyes. "Is that how you've felt? Are you lonely, Tori?"

No, I'm fine. The words instantly sprang to her lips. Because she was so used to saying them. Telling others. Telling herself. Ad nauseam.

Until she believed it.

But she looked back at the past few weeks and how she'd obsessed about saving this building. For Nancy, for the birds. How she'd stumbled back inside from that curb and let the fear cripple her into inactivity until the very last minute when desperation drove her to stage today's protest. How she'd forced Nathan from her mind but couldn't evict him from her heart. How she'd convinced herself he'd betrayed her and that it was no more than she deserved.

Was she lonely? She lifted her gaze. "Not right now."

"I missed you," he said, simply.

"I felt close to you, knowing you'd grown up in this building.

You were everywhere I looked. Forcing yourself into my consciousness. No matter how hard I tried to shove you down."

His lips twisted for the first time since he'd come smashing back into her life. The way he'd entered it originally. "That's me. Pushy. I'm sure you'll grow to hate it."

"I'm sure I'll grow to love it." Then, as his pupils flared, she raced on before the heat stained her cheeks. "It's not like you're exactly getting a prize in exchange."

"In exchange? I thought you didn't want me anywhere near you in the future."

"I was angry. And frightened. I overreacted."

"I'm demolishing your building."

"I know. And the thought makes me sick. Literally." As it had done many times over the past few weeks when the anxiety had just got too overwhelming. She pressed her lips to his knuckles. "But that in itself tells me something. A building should not have that kind of power over me." She held his focus. "Or over you."

His chest heaved.

"It's an inanimate object, Nathan. As much a victim of your childhood as you are. It's not responsible for what happened to you, though you've been punishing it all this time. Maybe forgiving the building is one step closer to forgiving the woman who lived here?"

Blue eyes glittered dangerously. Then they jerked around the room and came back to hers, conflicted. "You want to stay that much?"

With everything in me. But that in itself was not reason enough. Not anymore. She shuddered and sat up straighter. "I want this for you. I want to see you exorcise the bad memories and replace them with good ones, rather than just create a shrine to your unhappiness. No matter what glittering building you erect in its place."

His nostrils flared. But then the icy confusion bled out of his gaze and left a wounded blue in their place. "The building's rapidly running out of people to make memories with. What are you suggesting?"

She tossed her head back. "Renovate it. Reinvent it if you want. Then invite everyone back and give it back its soul."

"What about you?" *Oh, so careful.* "How would you feel about all the disruption?"

She took a massively deep breath. "I won't be here."

His voice tightened. "You're going to take the new apartment?"

She shook her head. The very thought made her stomach roil. "No. I'm not that brave. Not yet at least." He looked as confused as she was uncomfortable. It had been a long time since she'd taken any kind of risk at all. Talk about starting with a doozy! She filled her lungs with the warm New York air streaming in the window. "I'm coming with you. To your place. Until mine is fit for habitation again. I think I'll be able to manage that as long as you're there. If that's okay with you."

She fortified her heart and waited for the awkward silence. The stuttered denial. The astonished laugh. But all she got was…

"Are you serious?"

A barb of pure pain sliced low across her soul. Humiliation hovered just at the periphery of her mind, gleefully rubbing its hands together. Tori from yesterday would have cringed and accepted whatever knock was her due. Tori today shook her hair back out of her face and held his eyes. "Deadly. But if you're not interested—"

His hand shot out and stopped her from scrabbling to her feet. He stared at her, incredulous. "I meant, do you seriously think I'm letting you out of my sight once I've had you for my own? There's no way you're moving back in here."

For my own. Her heart set up a relentless thrumming.

"I like Morningside. And old habits die slowly." Surely he'd understand how difficult this was going to be at first. There was a time that a move would have excited her, not filled her with dread.

He read very clearly between the lines. "Then I'll come back with you."

Hope welled unfamiliar and rusty in her chest. "You hate this building."

"I'd have a different…lens now."

What was he saying? The hammering intensified. "You'd go insane in my tiny apartment."

Inspiration blazed bright in his eyes. "I'm not thinking about your apartment. I'm thinking about a super-apartment up on twelve. We can merge the west end of the building. Give you those park views you wanted."

"Not Nancy's place?"

Nathan frowned. "Nancy Smith was the closest thing to parenting I got, growing up. Maybe it's time I tried to be a better son to her." He smiled. "That's if you don't mind us looking out for her."

Tori kneeled up and clasped his hands. "She can stay?"

"Until she wants otherwise. She might have to move into your place while the renovations on her floor are happening. Do you think she'll manage?"

"The question is, will you manage? Can you do this?"

"*We* can do this. Together. It's not going to be easy for either of us but a demon shared is a demon halved, right?"

Old anxieties surged forth. "What if we get it wrong?"

"Would you rather not try?"

She stared deep into those eyes and borrowed his courage. "No. I'm through hiding."

He pulled her forward into his arms and she braced her hands against his scorching chest as his lips branded hers. Her already swimming head spun at the first touch of lips she'd thought never to taste again.

"But for the record…" he said, as they surfaced for air. "We're not getting it wrong. This is about as right as I can imagine. I love you, Tori. In my own messed-up, dysfunctional way. I love your honesty and your vibrancy and, beneath it all, your courage."

The slope of a vast uncharted rock face loomed before her. One part of her shied away from the unfamiliarity of it all. But an older part—a braver part—remembered how it used to feel to discover new mountains. Her pulse pounded and her blood filled with bubbles of joy. "It takes one to love one. And I do love you. So much."

"Enough to commit to a future together?"

"What exactly are we committing to?"

"Each other."

The hands that squeezed hard around her heart protecting it, unfolded like a lotus, letting the muscle leap and surge back to full blood flow. "Forever?"

"Hey, if I'm ripping down walls for you, I need a long-term commitment."

"Is this a proposal?"

"This is a job offer. I'm going to need someone to manage the building and tenants for me. Someone I can trust not to let the place rot."

She pretended to think about it longer than the nanosecond it really took. The opportunity to have purpose again… "That sounds like a reasonable trade." Her eyebrows shot up. "Oh, my God…I just realised. The boy who started the whole trading thing—was that you?"

His smile broke her heart. "When you have nothing you tend to get creative."

"You're preaching to the choir."

"Viktoria Morfitt, your days of having nothing are gone. If nothing else, you will always have me."

She took a deep breath. "Again…is this a proposal".

Please. Say yes.

"This is a promise. When I propose I'm going to do it properly with a ring and champagne. Not on a manky carpet surrounded by broken glass with an angry mob waiting down below—"

"Oh!" Tori pushed out of his hold and surged to her feet. Her surprisingly steady, optimistic feet. "The protest!"

She raced to the window and used the curtain to shield herself from injury as she boosted back out onto the ledge. She pulled herself carefully to her feet but smiled back at Nathan as she felt his strong hands curl around the waistband of her climbing pants tethering her to him more surely than any metal fixing.

They'd lost some of the crowd but the majority was still there. They all snapped their faces skyward as she reappeared on the ledge her hands raised and their chants of "Save the falcons, save the building," petered out expectantly.

Tori took a deep breath and yelled down to them. "The building stays. The falcons stay."

A surge of energy burst up from below as the crowd roared with elation. Tori almost stumbled at the wave of positivity that buffeted her like a rising thermal current, but Nathan's hands kept her secure. As she knew they always would.

She turned back to look at him, at that gorgeous, twisted smile he got when he was feeling particularly pleased with himself. But this time she understood. She felt it, too.

As the sounds of wild cheering rippled through the streets, two brown shapes exploded from above into the sky, disturbed from their happy nest. Wilma and Fred soared upward, then turned and dive-bombed down a few floors before wheeling right and coming back up past Tori.

As though they were waiting for something.

And then it happened. Two more shapes, smaller, slower, infinitely less proficient, joined their parents on the warm, summer air and the four of them twisted and soared and wheeled toward the Hudson and the rich pickings of the pigeon-rich bridges.

Tori leaned back into the strength of Nathan's grasp and let her imagination take her. It was as though the falcons departed with the demons that had haunted his building—their lives—leaving it clean and pure and ready for a new beginning.

0611 Gen Std HB

JULY 2011 HARDBACK TITLES

ROMANCE

The Marriage Betrayal	Lynne Graham
The Ice Prince	Sandra Marton
Doukakis's Apprentice	Sarah Morgan
Surrender to the Past	Carole Mortimer
Heart of the Desert	Carol Marinelli
Reckless Night in Rio	Jennie Lucas
Her Impossible Boss	Cathy Williams
The Replacement Wife	Caitlin Crews
Dating and Other Dangers	Natalie Anderson
The S Before Ex	Mira Lyn Kelly
Her Outback Commander	Margaret Way
A Kiss to Seal the Deal	Nikki Logan
Baby on the Ranch	Susan Meier
The Army Ranger's Return	Soraya Lane
Girl in a Vintage Dress	Nicola Marsh
Rapunzel in New York	Nikki Logan
The Doctor & the Runaway Heiress	Marion Lennox
The Surgeon She Never Forgot	Melanie Milburne

HISTORICAL

Seduced by the Scoundrel	Louise Allen
Unmasking the Duke's Mistress	Margaret McPhee
To Catch a Husband…	Sarah Mallory
The Highlander's Redemption	Marguerite Kaye

MEDICAL™

The Playboy of Harley Street	Anne Fraser
Doctor on the Red Carpet	Anne Fraser
Just One Last Night...	Amy Andrews
Suddenly Single Sophie	Leonie Knight

JULY 2011 LARGE PRINT TITLES

ROMANCE

A Stormy Spanish Summer	Penny Jordan
Taming the Last St Claire	Carole Mortimer
Not a Marrying Man	Miranda Lee
The Far Side of Paradise	Robyn Donald
The Baby Swap Miracle	Caroline Anderson
Expecting Royal Twins!	Melissa McClone
To Dance with a Prince	Cara Colter
Molly Cooper's Dream Date	Barbara Hannay

HISTORICAL

Lady Folbroke's Delicious Deception	Christine Merrill
Breaking the Governess's Rules	Michelle Styles
Her Dark and Dangerous Lord	Anne Herries
How To Marry a Rake	Deb Marlowe

MEDICAL™

Sheikh, Children's Doctor...Husband	Meredith Webber
Six-Week Marriage Miracle	Jessica Matthews
Rescued by the Dreamy Doc	Amy Andrews
Navy Officer to Family Man	Emily Forbes
St Piran's: Italian Surgeon, Forbidden Bride	Margaret McDonagh
The Baby Who Stole the Doctor's Heart	Dianne Drake

0711 Gen Std HB

AUGUST 2011 HARDBACK TITLES

ROMANCE

Bride for Real	Lynne Graham
From Dirt to Diamonds	Julia James
The Thorn in His Side	Kim Lawrence
Fiancée for One Night	Trish Morey
The Untamed Argentinian	Susan Stephens
After the Greek Affair	Chantelle Shaw
The Highest Price to Pay	Maisey Yates
Under the Brazilian Sun	Catherine George
There's Something About a Rebel...	Anne Oliver
The Crown Affair	Lucy King
Australia's Maverick Millionaire	Margaret Way
Rescued by the Brooding Tycoon	Lucy Gordon
Not-So-Perfect Princess	Melissa McClone
The Heart of a Hero	Barbara Wallace
Swept Off Her Stilettos	Fiona Harper
Mr Right There All Along	Jackie Braun
The Tortured Rebel	Alison Roberts
Dating Dr Delicious	Laura Iding

HISTORICAL

Married to a Stranger	Louise Allen
A Dark and Brooding Gentleman	Margaret McPhee
Seducing Miss Lockwood	Helen Dickson
The Highlander's Return	Marguerite Kaye

MEDICAL™

The Doctor's Reason to Stay	Dianne Drake
Career Girl in the Country	Fiona Lowe
Wedding on the Baby Ward	Lucy Clark
Special Care Baby Miracle	Lucy Clark

AUGUST 2011 LARGE PRINT TITLES

ROMANCE

Jess's Promise	Lynne Graham
Not For Sale	Sandra Marton
After Their Vows	Michelle Reid
A Spanish Awakening	Kim Lawrence
In the Australian Billionaire's Arms	Margaret Way
Abby and the Bachelor Cop	Marion Lennox
Misty and the Single Dad	Marion Lennox
Daycare Mum to Wife	Jennie Adams

HISTORICAL

Miss in a Man's World	Anne Ashley
Captain Corcoran's Hoyden Bride	Annie Burrows
His Counterfeit Condesa	Joanna Fulford
Rebellious Rake, Innocent Governess	Elizabeth Beacon

MEDICAL™

Cedar Bluff's Most Eligible Bachelor	Laura Iding
Doctor: Diamond in the Rough	Lucy Clark
Becoming Dr Bellini's Bride	Joanna Neil
Midwife, Mother...Italian's Wife	Fiona McArthur
St Piran's: Daredevil, Doctor...Dad!	Anne Fraser
Single Dad's Triple Trouble	Fiona Lowe